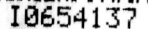

THE HIRONO CHRONICLES

THOMAS JOHN HOWARD BOGGIS

FIRST PRINTING, April 2021.
Harry Markos, Director.

Paperback: ISBN 978-1-913802-62-2
eBook: ISBN 978-1-913802-63-9

Book design by: Ian Sharman
Cover art and world map by: Mark Gerrard
Editor: Stephen Davis

www.markosia.com

First Edition

**THE HIRONO
CHRONICLES**
~ **SERIES** ~

BOOK ONE:
MEERA

BOOK TWO:
WOLF WARRIORS

BOOK THREE:
SPIRIT WAR

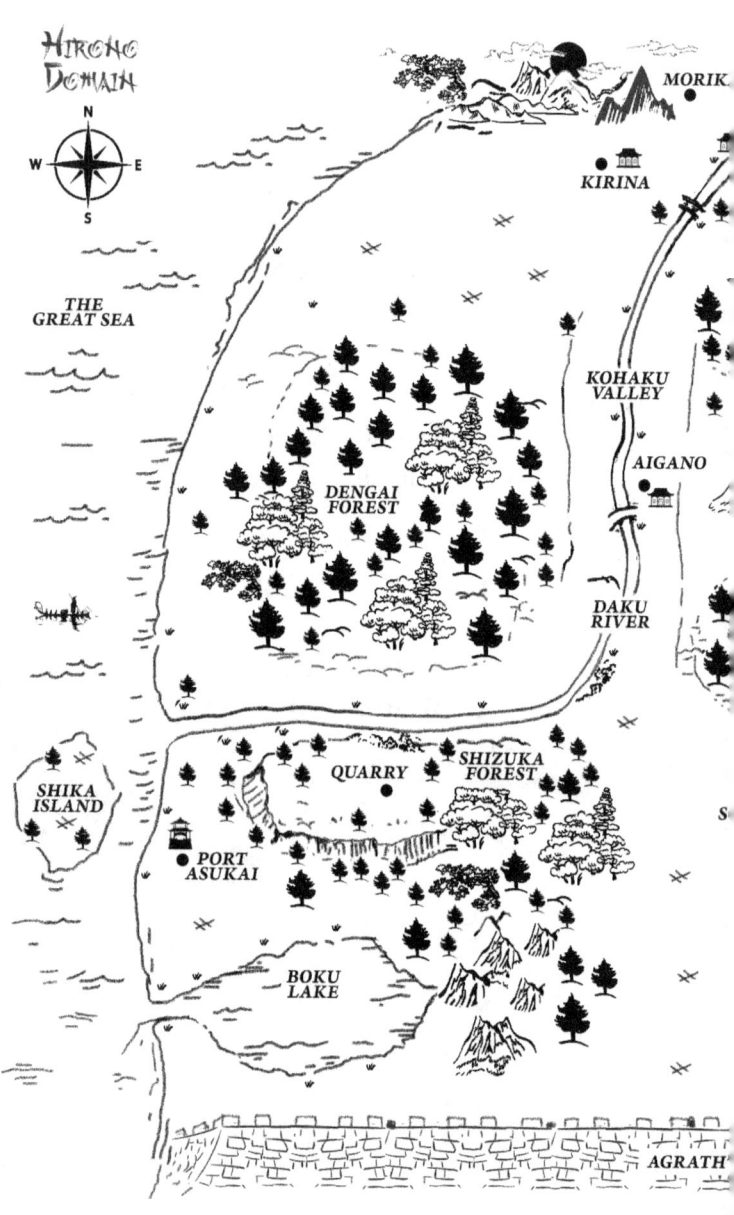

PROLOGUE

Cold. Cold to his marrow. Cold like he had never felt before. Cold that bit and gnawed, probed and wheedled, searching out any gap in his meagre clothing to pierce the soft flesh beneath. His arms were wrapped around his chest, desperate to keep in any warmth, so cold now that he feared they had frozen in place.

A bitter wind whipped around him sending stinging snow into his eyes and mouth, his teeth chattering so hard it made his head hurt and his eyes water, the tears quickly freezing on his numb cheeks. The wind blew harder, forcing him back: *Turn around*, it seemed to say. *Do not do this – you must go back*. But nothing would sway him from his task.

How long had he been trudging up this mountain? He could not remember; he had lost all sense of time as he struggled wearily on through knee-high snow, his legs no longer feeling like his own. He knew by now there would be no saving his feet – the frostbite would have put paid to them – but it did not matter. All that mattered was reaching the top.

He looked up but could still discern nothing ahead through the swirling cloud bank that cut off sight and muffled sound as effectively as a pillow over his head.

It cannot be much further, he thought. *It cannot be much further...*

Throughout this whole perilous journey, when so many others would have given up, one thing had driven him – shame. He wanted an end to this feeling, he *needed* it... He needed to take the shame that tore at his soul and turn it into anger, turn it into action, and bring about retribution on those who had wronged him.

It was this shame that forced his numb limbs to take step after painful step up the mountain, his body now encased in his frozen kimono like a carapace.

Shaking so violently he was liable to fall over, he looked up once more and saw a curious sight through the shifting clouds – a red disc hanging wispily in the sky, staring down at him like a great malevolent eye. *The blood moon.* He was close.

With a burst of energy he surged onwards, cutting a trail through the deep snow as the clouds gradually parted around him to reveal an amazing sight. He was standing near the top of the mountain looking down upon a sea of cloud that covered the land for miles around, broken here and there by distant peaks like the tips of icebergs. But he did not have eyes for the beauty around him, his gaze was set upon a plateau a stone's throw from the summit.

With his strength failing he hurried on to the plateau where he stumbled to its edge and slumped to his knees in the snow.

'I've made it,' he rasped, the breath catching in his throat. 'Above the clouds where the Gods cannot see, beneath the blood moon...'

Broken and spent, he painfully unwrapped his arms from his chest and with his frost-blackened fingers reached inside his kimono and withdrew a knife embossed with his family crest. He turned it in his hands, feeling its weight. He had never seen combat before. Never taken a life. He turned the blade until he felt its point against his belly. He steeled himself.

'I will make them pay,' he said hoarsely. 'I will make them pay for what they did to us. I will take this shame and use it to bring an end to their world... I will do it for you... father...'

CHAPTER ONE

Breath rasping. Hearts pounding. Limbs leaden with fatigue. Their paws beat out a staccato rhythm on the hard ground, a rhythm that had become their whole lives. *Running. Always running.* It had been their dream once. He had promised her they would run away together; that they would simply run and run and see where their legs took them… but, instead of that life, instead of running free, they were being chased… For them, running had now become a necessity, not a choice…

A howl rang out to their right and they turned towards it, not daring to slow down, only for another to echo a response to their left – they were closing in…

They ran on, side by side, straight for a stretch of woodland up ahead, hoping against hope to lose them within. They entered the shadows amidst the trees and felt their world close in around them, the surrounding trees pressing in tightly – silent onlookers to their plight.

'I need a… I need a minute…' she said, stopping at the base of a huge, gnarled oak tree. He stopped beside her as she flopped down in exhaustion, scanning the nearby trees for any sign of a threat.

'We cannot stay here,' he whispered. 'We need to keep moving – we must not let them catch us.'

She looked up at him tiredly, hopelessly.

'Takashi, maybe we should…'

Crack.

'Hush, Meera…'

Takashi tensed and pricked up his ears, snuffing the air - something was stalking them.

'We have to move,' he hissed, nudging her to her feet.

'But Takashi, we…'

'No time – let's go!'

With Takashi chivvying her on, Meera began to run once more, her head swimming with exhaustion and a dead weight in her chest, dragging her down – the weight of futility…

They sprinted on through a carpet of fallen leaves, silent as shadows, aware of every sound and smell around them – but so were their pursuers… The only animal capable of confidently hunting a wolf, is another wolf…

Takashi was fairly slight for a wolf, his fur a dark grey save for his chest, legs and ears which were midnight black. Meera herself was only slightly leaner than Takashi and her fur was a much fairer shade of grey that made her deep amber eyes stand out starkly from her face. But they were not the wolves they once were – constant pursuit, lack of sleep and poor diets had weakened them – but it had not stopped them yet…

As they wove their way through the serried ranks of trees another howl rang out – it was eager, exultant, *they had found their scent…*

'They're onto us,' Takashi breathed. His ears swivelled this way and that. 'I think… I think there's a stream up ahead… If we can get to that they may lose our scent. This way!'

He changed course swiftly and Meera bumped against him, stumbling and almost falling. She looked over at him hopelessly.

'We cannot outrun them forever,' she said breathlessly. 'They are going to catch us.'

'I will not let that happen,' he replied, without looking at her.

She could see the determination in his eyes, hear the resolve in his voice… but she did not feel it herself. She knew her fate was coming. They had always known this could not last forever… she had just hoped for a little longer…

They loped on as the stream slowly came into view ahead, the quarter moon gleaming in the eddying water – a fractured reflection of itself like broken glass. They reached the bank and slid down into the stream with a dull splash, the shallow water only reaching their bellies.

Takashi looked left and right as he sniffed the wind – *which way to go?* Another howl to their left made up his mind.

'Follow me!'

Takashi splashed off upstream with Meera hurrying to keep up, stumbling on the slippery rocks underfoot and feeling the current pulling her back.

'Takashi! Takashi, stop!'

'If we stop, we're done!'

'Then… then I'm done!' she called after him.

Takashi skidded to a stop in a spray of water and turned to face Meera, who was standing still in the middle of the stream.

'What… what do you mean…?' he asked in bewilderment. 'We cannot give up now, not after everything we've been through!'

'It is time…' she whispered back. 'It is time to stop running.'

'You cannot mean that,' he breathed, taking a step nearer. 'I promised you a life together – if we just keep running a little longer…'

'This is no life!' she cut across him. 'This is no way to live! We are hunted – will always be hunted – unless I return.'

'If you return, they will keep you from me,' he whispered. 'You know that…'

'Then at least one of us will have a chance at a life…' she replied.

'I do not want to live without you,' he said brokenly.

From amidst the trees on the banks behind Meera, shadowy forms began to emerge and prowled slowly towards them.

'You will have to find a way, my love,' she whispered back. 'For both of us…'

The wolves encircled them, glaring down at them from the high ground on the stream banks. Snarling, Takashi moved closer to Meera, shielding her from them – they would not get her without a fight.

From amongst the ranks a familiar face appeared, the other wolves backing away respectfully. The wolf was large, much bigger than Takashi, and from the tip of his snout to his tail ran a distinctive stripe of black fur. On his left shoulder were three deep scars around which the fur had never grown back. Takashi regarded him cautiously.

'She is not going with you, Jaroe,' he said menacingly.

Jaroe looked down upon him with fury in his eyes.

'After all you did for us…' Jaroe snarled. 'I knew you loved her, but I never expected you to take her from us…'

'You speak of her like some object to be owned,' Takashi hurled back. 'I took her nowhere – she came with me of her own accord… and she does not have to return with you.'

'She has a duty,' Jaroe hit back. 'She is the Soul Channel… and no matter how much distance you put between us that will never change. Without her no more wolves will come into being and our Council will dwindle and die, leaving Hirono a much more dangerous place.'

'Then perhaps that is best,' Takashi spat. 'If you would prioritise yourselves over the freedom of another.'

'Sacrifices must always be made for the good of the many,' Jaroe replied calmly. He turned to Meera and his expression softened. 'Now, Meera, it is time you came back with us – the Council awaits. Would you follow us, please?'

His hackles bristling, Takashi took a step nearer Jaroe.

'She is not going anywhere with you!' he snarled, but Meera stepped between them.

'I can speak for myself,' she said quietly. She turned to look at Takashi.

'It is over, my love,' she whispered. 'It was a beautiful dream and we enjoyed it while it lasted, but like all dreams, there comes a time to awaken.'

She turned to Jaroe.

'I will go with you,' she said to him, her voice barely audible as she glanced back at Takashi, 'but in my heart I will always run with you.'

At this, Jaroe nodded at two wolves who slid down into the stream and flanked Meera as she climbed out. Takashi took a faltering step towards them but stopped as Meera turned to him from the top of the bank.

'It seems I am not destined to have free will,' she whispered. 'Someone will always hold sway over my life.'

She turned and walked away, flanked by her two guards. Jaroe watched her leave but he and his remaining comrades stayed where they were. Once he was sure she was out of earshot, Jaroe turned back to Takashi.

'You have done us a great service in the past,' Jaroe said coolly. 'So I will not have you killed.'

Takashi stared into Jaroe's eyes – there was something different about him. He was not the wolf Takashi had known. In the wolf tongue feelings are intuitively sensed; there is no ability for falsity or double-talk, everything was open and honest – there for all to read. From the feelings he was sensing, he could tell that Jaroe was angry, conflicted, but he could get nothing else from him, like he had closed himself off from the world. *What had happened to him?*

'But… if we ever see you again,' Jaroe continued. 'I will kill you myself.'

At a nod from Jaroe, five of the wolves made their way down into the stream as Jaroe turned and began to walk away.

Glancing over his shoulder, he spat: 'Send him on his way.'

With echoing howls, the wolves sprang and Takashi turned tail and ran. The response was instinctual, automatic, every step carrying him further from his love, further from the reason these instincts were driving him – his reason to live… Meera…

CHAPTER TWO

The sun shone brightly from an endless ocean of blue sky, marred only by a few wispy clouds like the crests of waves. On the steps outside his house, Kamari Shiro sat and looked out over the sweeping beauty of the Kohaku Valley – the place he had called home his whole life.

Kamari's home was situated on the lower slope of the western side of the valley, surrounded by ancient maple and cedar trees. It was a simple abode, single storey, with a few small rooms separated by paper screens and sliding doors and surrounded on all sides by a covered wooden veranda. He may have been running the village, but he did not see himself as better than the other villagers, and besides – he had never had fancy tastes.

His gaze slid south and took in the house of his old friend Takashi Asano further down the valley, now occupied only by Takashi's mother and his little sister Mia. He still found it hard to go over there, but made sure to check in on them at least once a day. He often wondered what had happened to his friend, or if he would ever see him again, but he knew these thoughts were not useful. *As long as he's happy,* he thought. *As long as they are together.*

To keep from thinking about Takashi, he traced with his eyes the shining majesty of the Daku River that split the valley north to south, its surface glinting in the sunlight like a ribbon of diamonds. His gaze passed over the ornate crimson bridge that offered passage from the west bank to the east where the main bulk of the village was situated.

Aigano village had been around for many generations. It had been built by Kamari and Takashi's ancestors – Deakami Shiro and Timaeo Asano; great warriors of their age who had battled through many hardships to found the village so many people now called home.

It was on the eastern bank that you would find, not only the housing for most of the villagers, but also the training grounds, rice paddies, animal pens and most importantly of all – the shrine to the Valley Spirit, the being who watched over the valley and ensured good health and plentiful harvests for all.

It pleased Kamari greatly to see Aigano as it now stood. When he had been younger the village had been a shadow of its former self, a mere handful of houses and animal pens and the shrine to the Valley Spirit a tumbledown ruin, all but forgotten by the villagers.

But, since the defeat of Zian Agran at his fortress and the release of his many prisoners, the population of Aigano had been greatly bolstered and houses now reached as far as the revitalised shrine at the southern entrance to the valley. For her part in the battle with Zian, Kamari's wife Ellia had been made a Kurai warrior, and so Aigano was now an official outpost of Harakima castle. But, to his shame, Kamari had done little to train the village to defend itself, as he had been kept so busy simply keeping things running smoothly. For Kamari, the village amounted to a lot of mouths to feed, but also a lot of willing hands to make it the peaceful and prosperous place it had been restored to.

Thinking about all the work it had taken to rebuild the village, Kamari looked down at his hands which were sun-browned and calloused from day after day of hard labour. *These look like the hands of a fifty-year-old*, he smiled, but in truth he was only a little over seventeen summers old.

He had been a stocky boy when he was younger, although always in peak physical condition. Now that he was running the village, he had moulded himself into the form he believed a leader should take and his physique was lean and muscular. His long dark hair was tied in a knot at the back of his head, his piercing blue eyes set above a jaw covered in a fine stubble that his wife Ellia hated but he rather liked; partly because of the response it evoked from his spouse, and they did so love toying with each other. She kept him on his toes every single day – it was one of the main reasons he loved her.

He had enjoyed these few moments of quiet reflection, but thinking about Ellia brought his present worries crashing down upon him once more. Ellia being Ellia, she was not worried at all and had shrugged off his concerns, but he couldn't shake the feeling, no matter how hard he tried.

'Still worried, are you?'

Kamari glanced around to see Ellia leaning against the door frame behind him.

'Still…' he replied. 'Always… It's my job to worry, so they don't have to,' he added, gesturing at the village. Ellia snorted sardonically.

'It *is* your job to worry,' she said. 'But only about things worth worrying about. Shadows and superstition should not concern you.'

'That's just it…' Kamari murmured. 'I believe it is more than that…'

Ellia left her post and moved to sit beside him on the step. Like her husband, she was seventeen summers old and her dark hair was pulled back in the warrior style. She was of a slight build, but trained with Kamari daily and was easily a match for him in terms of athleticism. She had never been described as beautiful as such – and would not have taken it as a compliment, were it given – but her grey eyes were alight with an intelligence and mischievousness that Kamari had fallen in love with.

'These… *figures* your witnesses say they saw, they are nothing more than roving bandits,' Ellia said once she had sat down. 'And I've told you what we do about that – we just post a few more guards at night and ensure the animals are securely locked up at all times. We are bound to attract the odd vagabond as we grow and flourish, but it should not unduly worry us.'

Kamari took her hand in his and smiled at her.

'I am sure you're right,' he said. 'It's just…' He looked away from her, out over the valley. 'The descriptions of the figures they saw were… odd… inhuman almost, and both witnesses described the same figure without prior knowledge of the other's report. And they were, scared… truly scared… I thought maybe they were drunk at first, but…'

Kamari looked down at the ground in front of his feet, his eyes clouded with worry.

'I… I cannot shake this feeling that something is coming…'

Ellia looked at him sceptically, then got to her feet and glared down at him with her hands on her hips.

'Well, you're right about one thing,' she began, 'you've got a smack on the head coming if you don't stop being miserable and go do something useful!'

With that she turned and disappeared back inside the house, leaving Kamari smiling to himself. She was right as usual, there was much to do and he couldn't just sit around all day. Before he set off for the morning's rounds, he decided to take a few more seconds to enjoy the sight of his two children – Takashi and Meera, both not even a year old – playing with their self-appointed nanny, Mia, Takashi's nine-summers-old sister. They were seated on the grass just down the slope from the house, watching as Mia blew the petals off dandelions and giggling uproariously.

Since their birth, Mia had barely left their side – she had never had younger siblings and seemed to relish the opportunity to show them the ways of childhood. In many respects, Mia had become a beacon for the village children, but it was nothing to do with her association with her brother Takashi and the stories that surrounded him – it was her strength of will and fierce resolve that won her the respect she held.

Getting to his feet, Kamari strolled down the hill towards them and patted Mia on the head as he passed.

'You keep them out of mischief, alright?' he said. She smiled back at him impishly.

'I'll try,' she replied. 'But mischief usually seeks me out…'

Kamari smiled at this as he continued on down the hill towards the bridge into the village. He had just set foot on its wooden boards when a voice hailed him and he spotted Shio Takami detach himself from a group of nearby villagers and approach.

Kamari surveyed him as he drew near – he was roughly the same age as himself and had a quick, intelligent look about him. He was the son of Yaram Takami who had been killed when Zian's mercenaries attacked Aigano; Kamari remembered them fondly as one of the few families who had remained loyal to the Asano and Shiro families when times had been hard before the rebuild of Aigano.

Shio had already proven himself to be a useful ally on multiple occasions – not least when they discovered the threat from Lord Shigako Kichibei last year and had been forced to leave Aigano, for he had been instrumental in leading the evacuation to Harakima castle. Kamari found that he was relying on him more and more to help with the day to day running of the village and had been considering the possibility of offering him a more official position.

'Shio, how are things today?' he asked as the young man approached.

Shio shrugged effusively as he looked around them.

'Nothing much to report; there have been some arguments,' he said, gesturing at the group of men he just left, 'over the ownership of a catch of fish, but other than that, fairly quiet.'

He glanced around, then took a conspiratorial step closer.

'Although, there was a report of another sighting…' he murmured under his breath.

'Another one?' Kamari replied worriedly. 'Who was it this time?'

Here Shio pointed at one of the houses on the edge of the village.

'It was old Shinji; his eyes aren't what they used to be, but his description was similar to all the others,' Shio said. 'I've managed to keep it quiet for now, but word is spreading about these sightings.'

Kamari let out a long, anxious breath as he thought, then he leant in close to Shio.

'Alright, first I want you to double the night guard – don't tell them why, just tell them I said so,' he began. 'Second, I want patrols at either end of the valley throughout the day until the night guard takes over. Lastly, the animal pens – I want you to…'

At that moment a sudden commotion from the south end of the village cut them short. Shouts of alarm, splintering wood and animal roars reached their ears and they turned in bewilderment towards it.

'What on earth…?' Kamari whispered. With a worried glance at each other they sprinted off towards the source of the noise, dodging several villagers who were fleeing panic-stricken before it. Kamari tried to grab one of them to ask what was going on, but they were all too terrified to stop.

Rounding one of the store houses, Kamari and Shio just managed to avoid being trampled by an ox that tore past them and crashed through a wooden fence housing a number of chickens that leapt squawking into the air.

Before they had chance to react, three more oxen careened towards them from their pen, trampling roughshod through the rice paddies, heads down, nostrils flared, snorting with wild rage. In the shadows of a building just across from their position, an elderly villager stood huddled in fear, but when he spotted Kamari and Shio his face lit up and he began to hurry towards them, neglecting to check the way was clear. It was a fatal mistake.

Kamari could see what would happen but was powerless to stop it. Before he could even yell a warning, the man disappeared under the pounding hooves of the oxen, his crumpled body rolling to a stop in the cloud of dust they left behind.

'Get after them!' Kamari yelled to Shio over the hubbub. 'I'll check on him!'

Shio nodded and hurried after the oxen while Kamari rushed to check on the fallen man. He knelt beside him and checked his pulse. As expected. There was no way a man his age could have survived that.

Kamari looked up to see the carnage the oxen were wreaking on the village. The chicken coops were devastated, several houses had already been badly damaged and a small fire had broken out where a panicked villager had dropped a torch. Glancing round, he noticed that several villagers, led by Shio, had now gathered to try and catch them with ropes, but they were powerful beasts and, in this state, practically unstoppable. He recalled a time when he was young that he and Takashi had caught a rampaging ox, but this was different... There was only one way to end this.

Kamari drew the sword he always kept at his side and felt its balance in his hand. It was a katana – a two handed weapon with a long, slightly curved blade, the handle wrapped in delicate silk and the guard finished with an intricate pattern. He had not had to wield it for some time – had hoped never to need it again – but always kept it with him, just in case...

With his face set, he hurried towards the closest of the oxen that was hemmed-in by five men with ropes. As he approached, the beast lowered its head and dashed at one of the men. The man – more by luck than judgement – managed to dive to one side at the last second, leaving it to crash into a nearby house, caving-in the front wall. The animal shook itself and turned back towards the men, only to find Kamari standing there instead.

Kamari could see the hot breath clouding from its nostrils as it pawed the ground, readying to attack. He took up a fighting stance, his sword pointed towards his target, and waited... With a bellow of fury, the ox charged him, head down. When it was a mere pace or two from him, Kamari spun aside and brought his blade slicing down on the beast's neck. It was a clean blow and the animal dropped to the dirt without a sound.

Without wasting a moment, Kamari looked up to see where the other oxen were and within an instant had assessed the scene. Two of the oxen had disappeared north out of the village and were no longer a concern, but the other had cornered a young boy of about five summers while his mother looked on, screaming. Several villagers were trying to distract it, but it seemed fixated on its target.

There was no time to think. Kamari started running towards it and as though it had heard his thoughts, the beast began to run too, straight at the boy... As it neared its target, the animal swiped with its horns, but instead of striking a killing blow, it hooked the boy's kimono and hoisted him off the ground, yelling in terror.

Seemingly taken aback by this development, the ox began to buck up and down, trying to detach the boy who was shaken around like a ragdoll. When he was a few paces away, Kamari leapt at the bounding, thrashing beast and landed on its back, gripping it around the neck with his legs. Holding his sword one-handed, he sliced through the back of the boy's kimono, freeing him from its horn and catching him by the arm with his free hand as he fell.

Rather than calming down, the ox thrashed around more than ever with Kamari's weight upon it and began to thunder towards the river. Still holding the boy by his hand, Kamari chose his moment carefully and swung him to one side where he landed safely on a pile of hay, looking dizzy but otherwise unhurt. Kamari caught a glimpse of the boy's mother rushing over before he returned to his current problem – the rampaging beast he was riding.

With his sword still gripped tight, Kamari raised it high – seeking a killing blow on the ox's neck – but it seemed to sense his intent. As Kamari swung his weapon down the beast jerked its head back, the sword clashing with its horn and flying out of his hand. Now defenceless, Kamari knew he should let go but was transfixed with horror at what he had just seen.

Its eyes, he thought. *What is wrong with its eyes?*

What he saw when the ox turned its head still plagues his dreams at night, for where there should have been the simple, doe eyes of a domesticated animal, there was instead nothing but endless, roiling darkness – two bottomless pits to the unknown.

What on earth is this...? Kamari wondered fearfully. *Something is terribly wrong here...*

Snorting with exertion, the beast approached the river and Kamari realised at the last second what was happening. Without another thought he sprang from the ox's back and tumbled to the ground, shielding his head as he rolled to a stop in the dirt.

Kamari staggered to his knees and turned to watch as the ox stampeded towards the river... and toppled into the water. Crawling painfully towards the bank, Kamari was just in time to see the ox disappear beneath the surface, leaving nothing but a rapidly diminishing trail of bubbles to indicate its passing.

Kamari rolled onto his back and lay panting in the dust, frantically trying to process everything that had just occurred, but was too shaken to do so. One thing, however, was *very* clear to him – his feeling had been correct...

Something was coming, and it would be up to him to figure out what it was...

CHAPTER THREE

Where do I go now...? he thought. *What do I do...?*

In the weeks since he had been chased away by the wolf Council, Takashi had been wandering the wilderness, alone and broken, plagued by these questions he could not even begin to form an answer to.

The final pursuit by the Council had taken its toll on his already spent body. The relentless wolves had chased him for several hours across fields and forests, only stopping when the exhausted Takashi lost his footing and tumbled into a narrow gorge they could not safely jump into. There he lay, weak and bleeding, until the dawn of the following day when he finally dragged himself to his feet.

He could not say what it was that made him get up, for what did he have to go on for? He had lost Meera again, and that thought opened a hole in his chest he knew could never be filled. But still, for whatever reason, he had pulled himself up and continued to walk – but where he was going, he had no idea.

By this point, weeks later, he was limping badly. The fall into the gorge had injured his back foot and he had done nothing about the wound – he just could not bring himself to care. Without Meera by his side he was no longer sleeping and had all but given up eating, leaving him a gaunt and hollow shell – a ghost of himself, left to wander the world aimlessly.

And aimless he was.

For as long as he could remember, across his old life to his new, Takashi had always felt something pulling at him. He could never quite describe it, not even to himself, but it was some feeling of… *inevitability*. Destiny, fate, in his mind these words did not quite cover it, but whatever it was, it had always guided him. This feeling had helped him make decisions on countless occasions to keep him inching along his path towards whatever awaited him.

But since being parted from Meera that feeling had vanished and it was devastating – like losing one of your senses. He felt blind without it, lost and helpless. He had been separated from her before and had felt adrift and disconnected, but the feeling had always been there to show the way – like he was being swept down a river. This time was different… this time was so much worse… Now there was no river, no current, nothing to give him direction; he was floating in an infinite void with no landmarks in sight to guide him.

He had never felt so alone.

Ever since he had lost his pursuers and regained enough clarity to think, he had seen options scattered around him like fallen leaves, whirling and tumbling on a whim. But without the feeling to aid him he felt paralysed to do anything with them; unable to make any choices one way or the other, crippled by indecision and a single, nagging fear – *what if I make the wrong choice?*

A wave of light-headedness washed over him, and he staggered and almost fell, the options and choices swirling round his mind like a hurricane. He could risk it all, he could put his life on the line, he could throw caution to the wind and go back to the Council and… and… do what…? He could try to break Meera free and escape so they could run together again, but what if she did not want to leave? Perhaps he could try to reason with her? But… would that work? In the end it had been her choice to go with Jaroe; the weight of her gift and the futility of running from it was the reason she had given up, and nothing had changed on that front. Jaroe was right – she was the Soul Channel, and that wasn't about to change any time soon.

The more he thought about it, the more he began to wonder whether the only choice to make was… to do nothing. His whole life had led him to this point, and it was at this moment that the feeling that had guided his every decision had abandoned him – perhaps this was how it was meant to be? Perhaps he was not meant to be with Meera. Perhaps this was indeed the point where their lives parted ways forever. Something her father, Lord Orran, had once said to him suddenly surfaced in his mind:

'If you had never come here, she would still be alive.'

He was referring to her death before she returned as a wolf, and he later took back his words, but perhaps, in some way, he was right… Since the battle with Lord Kichibei and their flight from the Council, she had not been truly alive… As she had said herself, being hunted was no way to live. Perhaps, if Takashi made the decision to do nothing, she could make a life for herself with the Council and be happy, free from foolish notions of running away.

From the mists of his indecision a smell suddenly snapped him back to the present. He tensed and sniffed the air, thanking his lucky stars he was downwind. He breathed in the scent, forming a picture in his mind of the source. It was familiar, and unwelcome… wolf…

As little as he had cared for his own health and wellbeing over the past few weeks, it was still instinctual for him to keep out of the territory of other wolves, and he knew he had been careful to do so. That could only mean one thing… the Council had sent someone after him…

Takashi looked about and realised, as he often did these days, that he had no idea where he was. He was in a forest of cedars that reared from the earth all around him and away to his right was an open clearing carpeted in fallen leaves and lit by a shaft of sunlight that lanced down through the foliage above.

Glancing quickly around, he darted silently towards a large bush at the base of a nearby tree.

Once inside, he hunkered down and turned to face the other side of the clearing, where the smell was coming from. He snuffed the air again; it was getting stronger – his adversary was approaching...

He watched, tense and alert, and did not have long to wait... A few moments later a wolf appeared across the clearing. It was a male wolf, younger than himself, but something about his posture gave Takashi pause – he did not move like he was stalking a target. He moved with urgency, but it was more from... eagerness... or excitement...

The wolf stopped in the centre of the clearing and sniffed the air, lit fully by the ray of sunshine. He was a little smaller than Takashi but in significantly better health. His fur was a brownish grey but with a dull red patch on the back of his neck that caught the light. As Takashi looked closely, he realised that the wolf had mismatched eyes – one blue and one green – that scanned the area keenly, presumably for him.

A moment later the wolf began to move again, and he was moving straight for Takashi.

Has he smelt me? Takashi wondered. *Is he coming here right now to kill me?*

Takashi did not have long to ponder this, for the wolf was almost upon him.

He is sure to find me, Takashi thought quickly. *I must strike first.*

When the wolf was but a pace away, Takashi lunged at him out of the bush. They tumbled end over end in the fallen leaves and at last came to a stop with Takashi pinning the other wolf on his back.

'What do you want?' Takashi snarled. 'I did what Jaroe said, I stayed away! Why are you after me?'

The wolf looked up at him fearfully and began to stammer a response.

'I… uh… I'm sorry I startled you…' he began. 'Although in truth it was more you who…'

'Talk!' Takashi said, cutting him off and pressing down harder.

'I'd love to,' the wolf said in a strangled voice. 'But it's a little difficult with you…'

Takashi growled but did not release the pressure. The wolf took the hint.

'My name is Kaito,' he said. 'I was sent to find you by the Council…' Here Takashi pressed down harder than ever and Kaito struggled to get the next words out. 'But I'm… not here to hurt you, please… I just want to speak with you, please…'

With one last deep, low growl, Takashi relented and stepped back to allow Kaito to roll onto his front. For a few moments he simply lay there gasping for air, then turned to face Takashi.

'You never truly appreciate air until you're struggling to take it in,' he said hoarsely. 'If that's how you say hello, I'd hate to see how you say goodbye.'

'You said you came here to speak, so speak,' Takashi said menacingly.

'With pleasure,' Kaito replied with a weak grin. 'Usually all I hear from the others is them telling me to shut up.'

'You'll be hearing worse from me if you don't say something useful soon.'

'Point taken,' Kaito replied. 'Although you may not like what I have to say. It's about Meera…'

Takashi's world closed in around him.

'What's happened?' he breathed. 'What's wrong with her?'

'Well…' Kaito began slowly. 'To be honest with you, we're not exactly sure… No one has ever seen anything like this before. All we can say for sure is that she's… she's waning…'

'Waning?' Takashi replied in bewilderment. 'What do you mean?'

'She's…' Kaito faltered. 'She's getting weaker by the day, she's… dying…' he trailed off.

Takashi's blood ran cold.

'But I only saw her a few weeks back,' he whispered. 'How could she be…?'

Kaito got to his feet and shook the dust from his coat.

'The elders think it might be something to do with her rejection of the gift,' he said. 'It is like… the light of the Soul Channel is growing dim… It is the only thing that makes any sense. Since the battle with Kichibei there has been only one new wolf born – other than yourself – and for the first time in our history, he did not survive the transition, he… he died…'

Kaito dropped his gaze and a tinge of hopelessness entered his voice.

'Jaroe is worried,' he said anxiously, 'the Council is worried.' He looked up at Takashi. 'I am worried. If something is not done to fix this, it could spell the end of our Council and the enemies of Hirono will have one less barrier in their way.'

Takashi's mind was a blur of thoughts and emotions, so much so that he could barely form a sentence, but with an effort he managed it.

'So, how do I figure into this?' he asked. 'Why has Jaroe sent you looking for me?'

'Well, to be honest it's because we are out of ideas,' he replied. 'The elders have tried everything they can think of and nothing has made any difference. The only thing they haven't tried yet is the one thing Meera has been requesting for days… you…'

Takashi's heart leapt – *could this be a chance to see her again?* – but then it dropped like a stone. This could all be a trap, a way to lure him back. But if Jaroe had wanted him dead, he would have killed him at the river…

'Jaroe said he would kill me if he ever saw me again…' Takashi said slowly.

Kaito looked a little uncomfortable at this and for a moment seemed unsure how to respond.

'Yes, we – or should I say most of us – were a little taken aback by that…' he began hesitantly. 'Jaroe has not, uh… not been himself of late… He has taken to roaming the forests alone for hours at a time and houses himself away from the rest of the Council. He has become quick to anger, his retribution swift, and many of the Council are beginning to question his judgement...'

'That does not sound like the wolf I knew,' Takashi replied.

'It is not the wolf he is,' Kaito murmured quietly. 'He just needs to remember that. I am hoping that if you are able to help us... it will help him too...'

Takashi considered the younger wolf a moment. He wanted so badly to believe him, but this whole conversation had made him recognise something else he had lost. With the loss of the feeling that had guided his decisions, he now realised he had also lost the ability to intuit the emotions of other wolves. Normally he would have known instinctively whether Kaito was telling the truth, or whether there was any malicious intent behind his request, but in his present state he could read nothing more than the face value of his words.

He would have to make a choice.

Unbidden, a thought sprang to his mind. When he was younger and struggling with his insomnia, Takashi had often lain awake at night reading books and scrolls from the greatest minds of the age. As Kaito's appeal and all Takashi's previously considered choices swirled in his brain, a passage from one of the most legendary swordsmen ever known seemed to dance before his eyes:

A warrior should come to all decisions in the space of seven breaths.

At that moment, Kaito took a step nearer and looked at him imploringly.

'So, Takashi… will you help us?'

Takashi's chest tightened. *Seven breaths…* He would need to make a choice…

In… Out… How do I know he isn't lying…? This could all be a trap… *In… Out…* But what if it isn't…? Can I take that chance…? *In… Out…* I could follow him there and as soon as I see an opening, break her free… *In… Out…* But is that what she wants…? Is that what I am meant to do…? *In… Out…* What if her illness is because I did not leave her soon enough…? Perhaps I am meant to leave her alone…? *In… Out…* What if… what if I make the wrong choice…? *In… Out…*

Looking a little perplexed, Kaito took another step closer to Takashi.

'Did you… did you hear me…?' he asked. 'Will you help us…?'

Takashi's mind was a maelstrom – seven breaths and he had not made a decision. He could not just stand there – he would need to decide one way or the other. He just needed to have a little faith…

'Alright,' Takashi said finally. 'I will go with you.'

Kaito's shoulders sagged with relief at these words.

'Thank you,' he said excitedly. 'I knew I would be the one to find you… No one believed me… but I knew. The same way I know that you will help her… I can feel it…'

Kaito moved to stand beside Takashi, facing south.

'You have travelled a long way,' he said. 'I was about to turn back when I found you. We are in Dengai Forest, north of the old quarry where the

Council meet. It will be a bit of a trek to get there, so we'd better get moving.'

Without waiting for a response, Kaito set off southwards.

'Do you know any travelling songs?' he called back over his shoulder as Takashi reluctantly, suspiciously, began to follow him. 'Or any good poems?'

'None leap to mind right now,' Takashi replied irritably.

'Nor for me either,' Kaito mused. 'Perhaps we can just talk then. Will you tell me about your past life?'

'I thought it was common practice for none to discuss their previous lives,' Takashi replied.

'It is, but I see no reason for it,' he answered. 'It is not vain or boastful to speak of the life you lived. I myself only joined the Council recently. I was situated at Yukato, a small outpost of Harakima in the south near Agrath's Deterrent, while the battle with Kichibei was being fought. We were too few in number for Orran to consider summoning and too green in experience to be worth the effort anyway. It was my first posting, and my last... I died helping stop a bandit raid. My comrades managed to repel the attack, but I did not survive it. I still do not understand why I was considered worthy to join the Council...' he concluded, a faraway look in his eye.

'So,' he persisted, turning to look back at Takashi. 'Tell me about your life.'

'I'm beginning to understand why everyone tells you to shut up,' Takashi said, unable to hide a wry smile.

CHAPTER FOUR

The eyes of the ox swam before his waking sight, their endless, suffocating darkness pulling him in. For days now Kamari had been unable to rid himself of the haunting vision of those eyes; he had tried meditation and prayer, physical labour and calligraphy, but whatever he did, they always managed to claw their way back into his subconscious. Each time they surfaced he felt his heart gripped by an icy fear as the memory of the pain and confusion he had seen in those eyes enveloped him.

Since that day he had tried desperately to rationalise what he saw. He had stayed up long into the nights reading books and scrolls, searching frantically for any clues to what he had seen, but so far none were forthcoming.

You know why that is, his subconscious whispered to him. *Because none have ever seen this to write about it.*

As much as he hated it, he knew it was true. He wanted so fiercely for the explanation to be mundane and simple, but he knew his original hunch was correct – this was something new; the beginning of something dark and terrible Hirono had never experienced before…

Thus far he had told no one, not even Ellia, of what he had seen – for how could he? Those who didn't believe him would think him mad and those who did believe him might panic. No… he would need to solve this mystery himself and find concrete proof before he could risk telling anyone about it.

Come on, Kamari, he said to himself. *You can figure this out. Come on, Kamari…*

'Kamari…?'

Kamari returned to the present with a jolt, feeling like he had awoken from a dream.

'I'm… I'm sorry, what were you saying?' he asked falteringly.

Kamari blinked unsteadily as he used the momentary quiet before the response to reorient himself. It was late afternoon and he was standing at the centre of the village, overseeing the repairs necessitated by the rampaging oxen. It was incredible how much damage they had done in such a short space of time. Three families had been displaced from their homes due to collapsed walls, one of the store houses had been badly damaged and leaked grain everywhere and the chicken coops and ox pens were devastated. They had managed to round up most of the chickens, but all their oxen had been lost and they would need to wait until next season to trade for more.

Sowing our next crop is going to be tricky...
Kamari thought.

With an effort, he forced himself to focus on the figure standing before him – it was Shio.

'I was just saying that we only have enough lumber to fix the houses for now,' Shio said. 'We'll need to spend a few days gathering materials before we can fix the store house and the pens.'

'That's alright,' Kamari replied. 'We won't be needing the ox pen for a while anyway, but make sure you gather all the spilt grain and get it somewhere out of the weather.'

'Already taken care of,' Shio smiled.

'Good man.'

Together, they surveyed the activity going on around them. Kamari marvelled at the spirit of the Aigano villagers. They had taken a hit, but they had not let it stop them. He watched as groups of men, women and even children pitched in together to get the village back to normal as fast as possible.

This is it... he thought. *This is all they have to worry about.*

He sometimes envied the other villagers. Life was much simpler for them. They did not have the burden of knowledge and responsibility that came with being a leader. Kamari knew that, as bad as it was, being a leader often meant being economical with the truth. Some used this as a method of control, but on the occasions Kamari had done so, it had always been to avoid causing undue pain or distress to those he held dear. That was why the truth of what he had seen would remain with him alone until he fully understood what it meant and how he was going to deal with it… or it became too dangerous to hide any longer…

Kamari and Shio watched as the villagers cheerfully went about their repairs, smiling at each other and chatting happily.

Soon their spirits may truly be put to the test… he thought. *I hope they are ready…*

At that moment a man in his mid-twenties wearing a dirty, stained kimono came haring up to them from the direction of the rice paddies. He stopped in front of them, holding his sides and panting for breath.

'Kam… Kamari!' he gasped.

'What is it, Akai?' Kamari replied worriedly.

'Come… come quick…' Akai wheezed. 'There's something wrong with the crop!'

Kamari and Shio shared an anxious look before they nodded at the winded man and followed him back to the fields.

It was unlike anything they had ever seen before.

'What on earth is it?' Shio breathed, handing it over to Kamari.

'I have no idea…' he murmured back.

They were standing in the drained rice paddies that stood in tiers up the eastern side of the valley, staring in bewilderment at the harvested rice plant Akai had handed them.

'They're all like that!' Akai said in consternation. 'Every last one!'

'They cannot be...' Shio whispered. 'That is our whole crop for the year!'

'You don't have to tell me that!' Akai wailed. 'But they are!'

He took the plant from Kamari and ripped it open.

'We cannot eat this!' Akai all but screamed. 'What are we to do?'

Kamari looked at the plant in Akai's hands. The sight almost made him sick. A thick, black, tar-like substance was spilling from inside the plant, pooling in Akai's cupped hands, staining his already dirty skin. As Kamari stared at the dark fluid, the eyes of the ox sprang unbidden to his mind.

They are connected... Kamari knew instinctively. *But how...?*

Kamari dropped his gaze and his eyes fell on something in the mud at his feet. It was a distinctive hoof print – ox. He recalled that the oxen had passed through the rice paddies during their rampage...

'Well...?' Akai insisted. 'What do we do?'

'The first thing you can do is to stay calm,' Kamari replied sternly. 'The worst thing we can do is spread panic. We have enough food to last us for now.'

'Yes, for now...' Akai muttered, somewhat cowed. 'But...' His voice trailed off as he looked past Kamari. 'Hey!' he yelled. 'I've told you kids not to play here!'

Kamari turned around to see a group of children about Mia's age – two boys and one girl – playing on the path beside the paddy. They looked at Akai sheepishly and were just beginning to slink away when one of the boys stumbled, almost regained his balance, then fell limply to the floor.

With gasps of shock, the children crowded around their fallen comrade and Kamari, shooting another worried look at Shio, hurried over to help.

'Move back!' Kamari ordered the other children as he slid to his knees beside the boy and lifted his head. 'Hey, can you hear me?'

The boy gave no response. Kamari drew back the collar of his kimono to feel for a pulse and jerked his hand away at what he saw, feeling like a block of ice had dropped into his stomach. There, on the boy's neck, just above the collar bone, a series of black nodules peppered his skin, one of which was leaking a dark, viscous fluid…

Kamari covered the boy's neck once more. He looked down at him, hesitating a moment, then picked him up in both hands.

'We need to get him to a healer,' he said to Shio, who was standing anxiously nearby next to Akai. Shio nodded and, without a word, began to lead the way back to the village.

'Is Tayo alright?'

They were just re-entering the village and the young girl had not stopped asking the same question.

'He will be fine, Mara,' Kamari replied again. 'Hush now.'

Mara complied, but would not stop pawing at her friend – reaching up to grip his hand as much as Kamari tried to stop her. As she reached up again, something caught his eye.

'Take him,' Kamari said, handing the boy to Shio. Once Shio had hold of him, Kamari knelt in front of her and took her right arm gently in his hands, praying that what he had seen was nothing more than a trick of the light. But it was not...

As he drew back the sleeve of her kimono, he saw the same black nodules pocking the pale skin of her forearm and the breath caught in his throat. Standing up quickly, he called after Shio who had already hurried off towards the healer's house.

'Shio, take her too!'

Looking back in consternation, Shio nodded – his face pale as a ghost.

'Go with them,' Kamari said to Mara as comfortingly as he could. 'It will be alright.'

She looked up at him wide-eyed, gulped, nodded, and scurried over to the waiting Shio. Kamari watched them go, his mind racing.

What did this mean...? he wondered. *Was it some disease the oxen had picked up and passed on? But how had it started and what kind of disease can spread between animal, plant and human...? And what would they do without the rice crop...?*

At that moment another terrifying thought hit him – both Tayo and Mara had played with his children only that morning...

Kamari burst through the front door of his home to find Ellia sitting in the main room playing with the children on the floor. Ellia looked up at him in surprise.

'I'm not sure you quite slammed that door hard enough,' she said. 'The walls are still standing.'

Without a word of response, Kamari rushed over to the children and began to check them all over – hoping against hope not to find what he was looking for, while Ellia looked on in bewilderment.

'What are you doing?' she asked.

He ignored her and continued to check his children's skin while they giggled uproariously, thinking this was some kind of game.

'Hey!' Ellia said, gripping him by the shoulder. 'Talk to me – what's going on?'

'I'm checking them…'

'I can see that…' she replied. 'Would you mind telling me what for exactly?'

Kamari did not respond.

'Hey!' Ellia said, more loudly now.

Still he did not respond and with that she slapped him hard.

'Hey, you don't treat me like this!' she said angrily. 'You tell me what's happening right now or I swear I'll…'

Kamari finished checking the children and breathed a sigh of relief as he turned to his wife.

'There is some kind of a… blight a… a sickness…' he said falteringly, unsure how to explain it. 'The whole rice crop is ruined and while we were at the paddies, Tayo collapsed and I fear he is somehow infected with the same thing…'

Ellia's face had drained of all colour and together they looked at the children.

'On the way back from the paddies I saw the same signs of sickness on Mara,' he whispered. 'Somehow it is spreading…'

Ellia caught her breath as Kamari looked away from her in consternation, for the first time realising what he had done.

I should not have come here, he thought. *I could be infected too…*

'We must check each other,' he said, to which Ellia mutely nodded.

Several minutes later they drew apart.

'I think we are safe for now…' he said quietly.

'But what about everyone else…?' Ellia whispered back.

She's right… he thought. *Who knows who is vulnerable or how far it has already spread…? Tayo and Mara may just be the first to show signs… Ellia has hit upon the truth I've been avoiding – I put my family before my entire community…*

'I am ashamed to say I thought only of you, my darlings,' he murmured. 'My duty is to the village – not to you alone – but how could I do otherwise…? I needed to know that you were alright.' Here he got to his feet.

'Now that I know you are, I will inform the village immediately,' he continued. 'I will tell you what I will tell them – stay away from the rice paddies and visit no one unless absolutely necessary. We need to find out how it is spreading…'

'Kamari!'

Kamari looked over his shoulder at the sound of Shio's voice from outside, then turned back to Ellia.

'I will be back soon,' he said. 'Please explain all this to Takashi's mother and Mia, but… from a distance…'

He stared into her eyes a moment longer then spun on his heel and quickly left the house.

'What's the news?' Kamari asked Shio once he had joined him outside. Shio shook his head hopelessly.

'The healer has never seen anything like it before,' he replied. 'He is treating it like a fever for now, but… he has no idea how to cure it. And there is something else you need to hear… Word has spread fast; the whole village already knows… about the children and the crop…'

Kamari growled with anger.

'Akai… that loud-mouthed waste of skin…'

'The villagers fear we are being punished for something,' Shio continued. 'They have gathered at the Valley Spirit shrine to beg for a reprieve.'

With a worried look, Kamari led him towards the bridge to the eastern bank.

'We need to explain the situation fast and disperse them,' he said. 'Until we know how this is spreading, we should avoid meeting in large groups.'

Together they hurried over the bridge and cut off south through the town towards the restored shrine.

It was worse than he thought. Almost half the village was there – young and old alike – mingling together side by side, offering gifts and prayers as they begged for salvation. The smell of burning incense hung heavy on the still evening air, catching in Kamari's lungs and stinging his eyes as he picked his way through the crowd towards the shrine, careful not to get too close to anyone.

As he walked, Kamari desperately tried to figure out what he was going to say – how could he allay the fears of an entire village when he had no insight to offer them hope? They knew almost nothing about this sickness, and without a clear path out of it, how was he to quell the panic that would surely grip them?

On reaching the front of the crowd, Kamari had to tread carefully between the piles of gifts arranged along the steps until he was standing at the top of the altar in full view of the gathering. He tried to make himself heard, but the fearful discussions and distraught prayers initially drowned him out. Looking around, he noticed a gong hanging from the shrine roof and, after a quick search, found the stick to go with it.

With all his might he bashed the gong and the deep, ringing crash echoed out across the valley and silenced the crowd in an instant, every face turning to stare at him with a mixture of hope and despair. Once he was sure he had their full attention, Kamari gripped the gong to still its final echoes.

Now, what to say... he thought.

'I am sorry this news spread the way it did,' Kamari began, his voice clear and strong. 'I take full responsibility, but things have happened fast and we have been rushing to keep up. As you have heard, we have been struck by some kind of... sickness... a blight that may have started with our oxen, but has certainly devastated our entire rice crop for this year.'

Anxious gasps were heard passing through the crowd like a wave.

'But, worse than that... it seems to have somehow jumped to humans and at least two children so far have been infected by it.'

At this there were further gasps and anguished moans from parents and for a moment Kamari considered omitting details of the black nodules – for he feared it would spread instant panic and paranoia – but in the end he decided to trust in his people.

'The first signs of this sickness appear to be black nodules on the skin,' he continued. 'So I must ask all of you to check for these as soon as you get home and if you find them, then please attend the healer immediately.'

Kamari held his breath as he waited to see their response, but besides a few wary looks passing amongst the crowd, they kept their heads admirably.

'I know this news is frightening,' he added, the power of his words rising with every second. 'But we have faced adversity before, and I know we can do it again! When Lord Kichibei's forces attacked our land and we were forced to flee to Harakima, we did not panic, we did not lose our heads, and we will not do so now! I trust each and every one of you to conduct yourselves with dignity, honour and respect while we work together to defeat this new threat to our community.'

Looking out over the huddled crowd, Kamari was pleased to see that so far no one had visibly panicked, but what he needed to do right now was disperse them quickly with a few simple rules to follow.

'So, until we know who is vulnerable and how this sickness is spreading, I must ask all of you to do a few simple things. One – stay away from the rice paddies. Two – stay indoors unless absolutely necessary, and three – avoid gathering in large groups. I will see to the dispensation of food personally – no-one will go hungry while I am in charge, that I promise you. Now please, return to your homes and remember – continue to pray to the Valley Spirit if you desire, but do not spend so much time looking up that you forget to look down. Be good to yourselves and to each other.'

With that, Kamari stepped down from the altar and sat upon the lowest step, watching as the crowd slowly dispersed – now keeping wary distances from each other – and made their way back up the valley to their homes. He looked around him at the gifts arranged on the steps and wished with all his heart that they would make the slightest bit of difference, but he knew they would not. This sickness was not the work of the Valley Spirit...

Dusk was beginning to fall as Kamari made his way back to his home along the eastern bank of the river, his mind buzzing with a thousand questions. He was just passing one of the houses near the centre of the village when something caught his eye and he stopped dead. A shape could be discerned in the shadow of the building's entrance – an area of deeper darkness that no light seemed to penetrate. He strained his eyes to see but could make nothing out clearly.

He was just on the verge of moving on when the shape shifted, detaching itself from the shadows. Kamari bit back a cry as the shape took form – something humanoid but hideous – and stole away from the house across the bridge, disappearing up the slope in the direction of Dengai Forest that covered the western side of the valley.

For several seconds Kamari stood frozen in silent horror. His breath came in short bursts as he tried to make sense of what he had seen, but he did not have long to think, for at that moment the front door of the house burst open and a woman appeared, carrying the limp form of a child. The woman was weeping brokenly and wailing in distress as her husband appeared behind her bearing a lantern and together they set off toward the healer's house.

Even from this distance Kamari could make out the black nodules on the child's skin and terror gripped his heart.

What he had just seen had confirmed his worst suspicions – suspicions his rational mind had tried to reject. This was no ordinary illness, this was unnatural, and not only was it unnatural, but he now knew it was targeted. It was clear that the reported sightings over the past few weeks had been true...

Something is doing this to us... he thought. *Something is intentionally spreading this sickness...*

CHAPTER FIVE

'This has taken much longer than I thought… When Jaroe asked for volunteers to find you he seemed pleased I stepped forward, but… I'm realising now he may have just wanted to get rid of me for a while… I've been finding him harder and harder to read these days, I… Hey…are you alright…?'

Kaito turned to look back at Takashi, who had stopped several paces behind him and seemed unwilling to continue.

'It's not much further, it… oh,' he said, as realisation dawned. 'Having second thoughts, are we?'

Takashi did not respond as he scanned the trees ahead apprehensively. They were in the northern end of Shizuka Forest and from the smells wafting on the wind, Takashi knew they were not far from the sandstone quarry where the wolves held Council.

'I promise no harm will come to you,' Kaito said, taking a reassuring step towards him. 'I would never be complicit in such deceit.'

A sudden thought struck him and he cocked his head to one side.

'Can you not… can you not sense I am telling the truth?' he asked.

Takashi could not and it terrified him. He had hoped that as they drew closer to Meera his senses might sharpen, but thus far they had not. Was Kaito lying to him about Meera's whereabouts, or were his senses truly lost? Whatever the case, every instinct screamed at him to run from here – for Jaroe had promised to kill him if they ever crossed paths again – but how could he run now with Meera supposedly so close at hand?

Takashi took a breath and was about to respond when several wolves materialised from amidst the trees ahead, making their way purposefully towards them. Kaito took a step forward as the wolves wordlessly surrounded them.

'Brothers,' he began. 'It is good to see you again. As you can see, Takashi has…'

'Jaroe wants to see you both,' one of the wolves said solemnly, cutting across Kaito. 'Now…'

Kaito looked back at Takashi, who was glancing warily from one wolf to the next, then moved to stand alongside him.

'Very well,' he replied. 'Lead the way.'

Quiet as shadows, the wolves began to escort them south towards the quarry with Takashi tensed and ready to flee at any moment.

'Talkative bunch, aren't they?' Kaito murmured.

'I don't think they like me very much…' Takashi replied.

Kaito was silent a moment before he responded.

'They are just afraid,' he said at last. 'Afraid for the future of our Council. It has hit everyone differently – some reacted with anger, others despair; for others still, it was a call to action. I fear you will hear a few choice words before all this is through, but please pay them no mind. It is not for others to comment on the actions of two souls in love.'

Those last few words hit Takashi as though from a great distance and echoed over and over in his mind. He realised then that he had never thought about his actions in that way; about his part in Meera's flight from the Council after the battle with Kichibei. He had felt neither guilt nor shame as he and Meera ran away together. Every step of the way until the Council came to reclaim her, he had been led by that feeling of inevitability – as far as he had been concerned, he was meant to be with her, and there was no guilt or shame in that.

But now the feeling had vanished it led him to question everything. Perhaps what he and Meera had done *was* wrong. Perhaps he *should* feel ashamed for his part in all this. Perhaps he deserved the angry glances his escorts were throwing at him. Maybe all he deserved at this point was to see Meera one last time, do what he could to help her, then be sent on his way.

But he just could not bring himself to believe that after everything they had been through to be together, it would end with guilt and shame and separation. Even though the feeling that had always guided him was gone, it did not mean this was the resolution it intended. He had made a choice, and that choice had theoretically brought him closer to Meera, and that had to mean something... Perhaps the absence of the feeling was a test...? But if it was, he had no idea what it was testing or why, or what he had to do to succeed... or if it was even possible to do so...

'We're here,' one of the wolves said, cutting across his thoughts, and at these words Takashi's heart skipped a beat.

Meera... I'm almost there...

The thought of seeing her again both terrified and excited him. If what Kaito had said was true – and this wasn't all a trap – then she was dying and had called for him to help, but what if he could not help her? What if he had to watch her die? Being separated from her was almost more than he could bear, but the thought of living in a world without her... that was an existence he knew he simply could not endure.

Ahead of him his escort had fanned out around an unseen edge and, as Takashi approached them, the quarry finally came into view. Surrounded by the Shizuka Forest, the sandstone quarry had once been mined extensively by a group of enterprising merchants and the resulting stone had been shipped around the world from nearby Port Asukai. The quarry itself was not particularly large, but it was deep and stepped down through multiple tiers to its base, around the edge of which were numerous caves cut into the soft stone.

Takashi recalled the first time he had seen this place. He had been sent west from Harakima Castle by Lord Orran to find the wolves and plead for their help in the battle against Lord Kichibei. After a nasty fight with a handful of bandits, he and Kamari had stumbled upon a group of wolves and been led to the quarry where they were holding Council.

At that first sighting, the quarry had been filled by rank upon rank of wolves as they desperately discussed how to retrieve Meera – their Soul Channel – after she had been taken by a southern lord, bent on stealing her gift for his people. He and Kamari – with the help of a captain they met at Port Asukai – had managed to save her, but the experience had been extremely hard on her. Takashi realised that he often forgot just how much she had been through in such a short space of time, and the thought clawed at his heart.

Looking out across the quarry now presented a much different scene from that first sighting, for instead of bustling with life, it was completely deserted and not a sound could be heard anywhere.

'Where is everyone...?' Takashi murmured to Kaito, who had appeared at his side.

'Most are out hunting or patrolling, some may still be looking for you,' Kaito replied under his breath. 'But in general, our numbers are not what they were. We lost

a great many during the battle with Kichibei and as I…'
Here he faltered a moment. 'As I explained before, we have
had no new wolves join our Council for some time…'

Takashi stared sorrowfully across the quarry, but
before he had time to respond one of their escorts
stepped forward.

'This way,' he grunted, as he began to slide down
the tiers to the bottom of the quarry. Takashi glanced
behind him once more at the open forest. He still
had no idea if this was a trap, but he had come too
far now and if there was even a chance he could see
Meera again, then he had to take it.

With an encouraging look from Kaito, he took
a deep breath and followed the escort down to the
bottom of the quarry.

They reached the quarry base in a shower of dirt
and stones and shook themselves vigorously as the
dust settled around them.

This is it… Takashi thought, as he surveyed the
steep walls surrounding him. *No way out now… This
is where I find out if…*

His thought was cut short as a scent reached his
nostrils; a familiar, well-loved scent that made him
catch his breath.

It cannot be… he thought. *She… She's really here!*

Without waiting to be invited – and drawing
angry snarls from his escorts – Takashi hurtled off,
following his nose straight towards one of the larger
caves cut into the quarry wall.

With his escort hot on his heels, Takashi burst through the mouth of the cave casting left and right for Meera, but was forced to skid to a stop in front of a hulking shape that loomed suddenly out of the darkness. As his eyes adjusted to the dim light, Takashi stumbled back in shock as he found himself standing face to face with Jaroe.

Jaroe had always been bigger than Takashi, but in that moment he seemed to tower over him, staring down with a look he could not begin to fathom.

'I was unsure if you would accept our invitation,' Jaroe said without preamble.

'Your threat was pretty clear last time we met,' Takashi replied guardedly.

'Yes, well,' Jaroe began, 'things have changed since then...'

At that moment, Takashi's escort – with Kaito close behind – came barrelling into the cave and skidded to a stop beside them.

'Jaroe, I'm sorry, he...' one of the wolves began, but Jaroe silenced him with a look.

'Please wait outside,' he said. 'You too, Kaito.' The escorts left looking shamefaced and Kaito dejectedly followed them.

'I have no doubt Kaito explained the situation?' Jaroe asked after they had gone.

'He did, at great length...' Takashi replied. 'I would not have come for any other reason.'

'Yes, he likes to talk that one,' Jaroe muttered, looking after Kaito before turning back to Takashi.

'Then you know why you are here. We are out of ideas, but she thinks you can help and the elder agrees – although his mind is not what it was…'

'If Meera is sick I want nothing more than to help her, but I'm not sure what I can…'

'Takashi…?'

Her voice seemed to fill the cave and cut straight to his core, the beloved sound flooding his mind with memories.

'Meera…?' Takashi called, trying to look past Jaroe.

For a moment Jaroe eyed him shrewdly, as though debating something internally, then he stepped aside to reveal Meera lying on a bed of leaves at the back of the cave.

'Meera!' Takashi rushed to her side and looked down at her, his heart bursting with joy and terror at once.

From her prone position, Meera looked up at him. She appeared drawn and haggard, her breathing shallow, but at the sight of him a light seemed to kindle in her eyes.

'Takashi, my love, I was beginning to think you would never arrive…'

At these words, guilt swirled in Takashi's chest – he could not believe he had even contemplated not coming here.

'I'm here now…' he replied, trying to keep his voice steady. 'Are you alright? What's happened to you?'

Meera was about to respond when she faltered and looked away from him. She took a breath and tried again, her voice trembling.

'I tried...' she whispered. 'I tried; I really did... I tried to accept it, to come to terms with it, but I... I...' She trailed off as she grappled with the words. 'I cannot accept another life that is not truly my own... I do not know why this gift was bestowed upon me, but I do not want it and I... I fear it is killing me...'

Takashi bit back a cry of anguish and tried to stay strong as Jaroe watched silently.

'I will not let that happen,' he said, with as much vehemence as he could muster. 'Kaito told me you thought I could help – tell me what I can do, and I will not rest 'til it is done.'

With an effort, Meera sat up so she was level with his eyes and stared into them lovingly.

'I made that up,' she whispered, and behind them Jaroe's expression darkened. 'I managed to get the elder to agree with me, but really I just wanted to see you one last time... I do not think anything can help me now...'

'That may not be strictly true...'

As one, they turned to face the mouth of the cave from which the voice had emanated. An elderly wolf stepped forward and Jaroe dropped his gaze respectfully as he passed.

'Kenjin,' he murmured. 'It is good to see you.'

Kenjin nodded at Jaroe as he moved stiffly towards Takashi and Meera and sat down beside them. The old wolf's fur was patchy in places and almost completely white, but his eyes shone as brightly as ever as he regarded them.

'You youngsters are so quick to despair,' Kenjin murmured as he looked at Meera. 'I told you things would be clearer when he arrived, and indeed they are.'

Meera looked at him in bewilderment.

'They… they are…?' she asked.

'Yes, it is most clear now,' Kenjin replied, as he looked from one to the other calculatingly. 'There is an old proverb that states: "One thing should never become two." The Kurai take this to mean that one should look for nothing more in the way of the warrior than what is already there – but I see now that it has another meaning as well…' He considered them both a moment in silence, then continued. 'Yes… yes that is what it is. It could never have worked…'

Takashi and Meera glanced at each other in confusion as Jaroe moved to sit closer to them.

'I don't understand…' Jaroe said slowly. 'What do you…?'

But Kenjin had warmed to his theme and ignored Jaroe's questions.

'In the normal course of things, when a Soul Channel nears the end of its days, a Transference is initiated,' he began. 'But this is not a normal situation and I fear a Transference will not occur in these circumstances. Ordinarily, a replacement is summoned and the gift is transferred – how they are chosen is not for us to question, but you have already experienced this yourself, Meera, though I doubt you recall any of it…'

'It is mostly a blur...' she replied slowly. 'Some time before the battle with Kichibei, I remember a force calling me, pulling me away from Takashi and I... I remember travelling into the west, but... no more... The next thing I knew, I awoke in front of the Council...'

'You were called to Sen'i,' Kenjin said excitedly. 'That is where the Transference takes place and that is where you must go now!'

'To Sen'i?' Jaroe said in disbelief. 'You cannot be serious...?'

'I am deadly serious,' Kenjin replied.

'Wait... what is Sen'i?' Meera asked, perplexed. Kenjin did not respond for a moment as a faraway look entered his eyes.

'Sen'i is what we call the spirit realm,' he said at last. 'It is a transitional place, a place all life must pass through on its way to the next. It is there you will find the Senzo...'

'Senzo? Who is that?' Takashi asked in a hushed tone.

'The Senzo has been around for as long as there has been life on this earth,' Kenjin replied. 'It would be a fool's errand to try and name his many deeds, but one you will know already – it was he who created the original Soul Channel...'

'The original Soul Channel...' Takashi whispered, unable to keep the awe from his voice. 'I met him... When I first awoke, he was there and it... it was my ancestor, Timaeo Asano...'

Kenjin looked at him oddly.

'I do not know what it was you saw,' Kenjin said slowly, 'for Timaeo has been gone a long time. But you are correct; he was the first, and on receiving the gift he went in search of a strong line of warriors and found the Kurai, forging the link between them and the wolves and beginning the legacy of the Transference.'

Kenjin stood up and moved to the mouth of the cave where he looked out across the quarry.

'It is the Senzo who initiates every Transference and selects every new Soul Channel,' he said, turning back to Meera. 'Whatever is happening to you, he must not be aware of, so I can see no other course of action…' Here he took a deep breath. 'You must venture into Sen'i, locate the Senzo, and beg him to transfer the gift to another before it kills you and the gift of the Soul Channel is lost forever.'

Takashi and Meera stared at him aghast while Jaroe looked on in shock.

'I must… I must do this alone...?' Meera asked fearfully.

'No, I would not recommend you go alone,' Kenjin replied. 'But it should not be a large group either, for you will need to travel fast. A large group would be more easily detected… and less respectful to the spirits…'

'Is it safe?' Takashi asked anxiously.

'It is not a place you would venture to in ordinary circumstances,' Kenjin answered. 'It is normally a one-way trip… Members of the Council have been known to visit there before, and many of them lost themselves… But if you go as a group, show respect and humility and stick to your purpose, I believe you will be alright…'

Kenjin turned his attention to Jaroe.

'You have been quiet, Jaroe,' he said. 'What say you? Do you still think my mind is not what it was…?'

On hearing his own words thrown back at him, Jaroe's shocked expression was replaced with one of shame and embarrassment.

'If I have caused you offence then I am deeply sorry,' he said humbly. 'As extreme an option as it sounds, I believe you are right – we have no other choices and time is short. Kaito!'

At the sound of his name, Kaito appeared like a flash at Jaroe's side.

'Assemble the Council,' Jaroe said. 'We need to select our group…'

It took some time to locate the full Council – as many were out on patrols or hunting – but soon they had all arrived and stood ranged around the many-tiered quarry, staring down at Takashi, Meera, Jaroe and Kenjin at its centre. Looking around at his brothers and sisters, Jaroe took a step forward and addressed them.

'Thank you for coming so swiftly,' he began. 'You are all aware of the crisis we face, so I will not explain it again, but there has been a development. Kenjin has devised a plan that could save us, but I must warn you,' here he cast an apologetic glance at Kenjin, 'it may appear somewhat far-fetched at first...' Jaroe took a breath before continuing. 'In order to save Meera and ensure the continuance of our Council, a small group of us are to venture into Sen'i to locate the Senzo and beg him to transfer the gift to another.'

At this, whispering broke out amongst the wolves, rising in volume so that Jaroe had to shout to be heard.

'It is our only remaining option, our one hope for this Council!' he boomed over the hubbub.

Questioning voices called out from all sides:

'What if you cannot find him?'

'What if you are too late?'

'What if you do not return?'

One voice, clear and calm, stood out above all others:

'Who is to be in this group?'

The voice came from a female wolf standing at the base of the quarry not far from Jaroe. She was large for a female and russet brown, save for white tail and ear tips. Meera craned her neck to see her and received a glance filled with fury and contempt for her troubles.

'That, Hina, is precisely why you are all here,' Jaroe replied. He turned and looked back at Meera.

'It is a lot to ask in your present state, but you must of course be part of the group,' he said.

'You can barely stand, are you sure you can do this?' Takashi asked, full of concern.

'I have to,' she replied in a hushed voice. 'Not just for me and the Council, but for you...' Here she turned to look at Jaroe. 'I will go… but not without Takashi.'

'They would have to kill me to stop me,' Takashi murmured at her ear. A snarl crossed Jaroe's face, but he knew there was no point arguing. He turned back to the Council.

'I will be the third member of the party…' he began, but at this further shouting broke out around the quarry.

'You cannot leave!'

'We need you here!'

'Who will run the Council in your absence?'

Jaroe ignored them all and continued speaking, his voice echoing around the sandstone walls.

'…and I am looking for two more to join us!'

A hush fell over the gathering as Jaroe looked from one wolf to the next, sizing them up, and finally settled on Hina.

'Hina, you will be the fourth member of the group,' he said. It was not a request.

'I would be honoured,' she replied, bowing her head slightly. She moved to sit beside Jaroe, but as she turned to face the Council she threw another furious, hate-filled glance at Meera.

Jaroe looked around the quarry once more.

'I need one other…' he began, but before he could finish his sentence Kaito had stepped forward and addressed him.

'Jaroe, if it would please you… I would be greatly honoured to join the group.'

At this, a tumult of voices broke out once again.

'Be quiet, you young pup!'

'Grown-ups are talking!'

But Kaito would not be deterred.

'I have done a lot of research into Sen'i,' he began, trying to make himself heard. 'I know I am fairly new to the Council... and I know I am not as experienced as many of the others, but I believe I could be of...'

Kaito's voice was drowned out once more by the angry, derisive shouting.

'He has barely seen combat...'

'He knows nothing of the world...'

'He is all talk!'

Ignoring the shouts, Jaroe regarded Kaito coolly. He could not quite figure him out. He was always just a little too... positive... a little too... keen. Something about him had always made Jaroe suspicious. Was he genuine, or was this all some flimsy grasp for power? Did he really want to help the Council, or was it just an attempt to climb the ladder? Just what courage was there in his soul?

Jaroe shook his head in an attempt to clear it. Recently he had been finding it hard to get a reading on anyone, his senses felt strangely off.

The mocking voices continued to call out.

'He will derail the whole venture...'

'He would talk your ears off...'

'He would only slow you down...'

With disparaging voices ringing out all around, Kaito took a step closer to Jaroe and looked at him earnestly.

'Jaroe, you can trust me... I... I just want to help...' he said.

The taunts continued and Jaroe barked a command: 'Quiet!'

As silence fell, Jaroe stared hard at Kaito and made his decision. He decided that if he could not read this upstart young wolf then he would test him, and like as not prove his immaturity and his cowardice...

'You would not have been my first choice,' Jaroe said slowly. 'But you may join us...'

At this, Kaito's face lit up, but the surrounding wolves snarled in annoyance.

'We have our group!' Jaroe called out, bringing quiet once more. 'And we have not a moment to lose. In my absence, I appoint Kenjin to be in charge...' Here he turned to Kenjin. 'That is, if you would honour me by accepting...?'

Kenjin nodded.

'Of course, just come back to us safe – all of you,' he said. Jaroe nodded back.

'Then it is settled, come!' he said to Meera, Takashi, Hina and Kaito. 'We leave at once!'

With that, Jaroe turned and began to scramble out of the quarry while the rest of the Council slowly dispersed, whispering and bickering amongst themselves. With a nervous glance at each other, Takashi and Meera followed after Jaroe with Hina and Kaito close behind.

On reaching the top of the quarry, they regrouped around Jaroe, who was looking off north through the trees.

'Our best chance of finding a doorway to Sen'i is in Dengai Forest,' Jaroe said. Without another word, he set off northwards and for a moment Takashi and Meera stood still and watched him go.

'Dengai Forest – well, at least we know which way that is, eh?' Kaito said brightly as he passed by Takashi on his left and followed after Jaroe. Takashi watched him for a moment, then turned to Meera.

'If at any point you want to stop or turn back, just say the word,' he said quietly.

'I fear it would be death to do so,' she murmured back. 'The only way is forward… Besides, I feel stronger already with you here.'

Takashi looked like he wanted to say more, then simply nodded and set off after Kaito and Jaroe. Meera was about to follow him when a low voice stopped her.

'It may seem like we are here to help you, but know this…' Hina said, appearing at her side with a snarl on her lips. 'No one in our long history has ever rejected the gift. Not one. You have brought us to a precipice, and I will not let us fall…' Here her voice dropped lower still. 'But what happens to you after…'

Her voice trailed off as, with one last hateful look at Meera, she followed after the others.

Meera watched her go; fear, confusion and shame in her eyes.

I am a monster… she thought, as she slowly began to follow Hina.

CHAPTER SIX

I knew their spirits would be tested, but this is worse than I feared...

Kamari sat alone, cross-legged in the darkened main room of his home, his arms resting on his knees in a meditative posture. His eyes were closed as though he were at peace, but beneath the lids they were darting around in agitation. Every now and then his hand would move to scratch his right forearm in an automatic manner, as though he were not aware he was doing it.

Kamari was desperate to empty his mind, to open himself up to ideas and possibilities on how to resolve this crisis, but all he saw were horrifying images from the last few days – the infected rice plant, the nodules on Tayo's neck, the eyes of the ox...

A great burden of responsibility sat squarely on his shoulders and he feared it would crush him... The whole village was looking to him to fix this, but he had no idea what to do or where to start. He had to find the source, he had to stop the spread, but how...?

At this point all he knew for sure was that it was something unnatural targeting them, and that was both a blessing and a curse... A blessing in that there was clearly intent behind this, and intent meant a sentient being – a being that could be reasoned with or killed – and a curse in that this sickness, being unnatural, had no known cure to slow or stop it... They had learned that the hard way.

It seemed that already, in the space of only a few days, most of the village children had now contracted the sickness to varying degrees. It was flu-like in its symptoms, but much more intense – bringing with it breathing difficulties and vomiting, as well as horrifying fever dreams that terrified the infected children and worsened their parents' anguish. And even though Kamari had told the villagers to stay home as much as possible, it had passed from one to another with frightening rapidity, and in the last day he had received reports of several adults catching it too.

Staying at home will do them no good... his mind whispered to him. *You saw what it was that is spreading this...*

The dark figure suddenly filled his thoughts, looming larger and larger with every second. Again he saw it stealing away from the house and again he heard the mother's cries of anguish as she carried the limp form of her child to the healer.

This is no simple sickness... his mind wheedled. *This is targeted...*

That may be true, he thought, *that creature may have started this and may be helping it spread, but I fear it may also spread like any other illness. Until I know for sure, I must keep everyone separate...*

His mind flitted back to that morning's patrol of the village. The sight of it had tugged at his heart. Gone was the hustle and bustle, the laughter and chatter, the ebb and flow of life he had loved so much. On his orders, each and every household had isolated itself from the others and the village now looked like a ghost town.

During his patrol, he had noticed families peering out at him from their windows wherever he went. He had felt their fear and frustration like heat on his skin. It uncomfortably reminded him of how Aigano had been before the rebuild and the business with Zian. The village had been going through a rough patch and the villagers – who in times past had held great respect for the Asano and Shiro families – had shown them nothing but disloyalty and anger. He remembered walking through the village back then and feeling their hostile eyes upon him.

These thoughts stirred up old feelings of indignation and anger at the disrespect shown their families, but Kamari had matured since then and had learned that respect is earned – it is not an entitlement. Since Zian and the rebuild, he felt for the first time that he had earned the respect of the Aigano villagers – both old and new – but after walking through the village that morning and feeling their anxious, desperate eyes upon him, he felt like he no longer deserved that respect.

How am I going to help them...? he thought again for the hundredth time. *How am I going to stop this?*

As he sat there, he felt his frustration build and wished that he had given more credence to the sightings of strange figures around the village. If he had paid them more mind and looked into it sooner then perhaps he could have... but no, he stopped himself. This train of thought would not help him. However, the investigations he had performed during that morning's patrol had earned him some new information.

He had made it his mission to have a word with every villager who reported a sighting and had asked each of them for as detailed a description as they could manage. He did not know what he was hoping to hear, but what he had discovered was that – while the descriptions were similar in many regards – there were several key differences that could not just be foggy recollection. This led him to believe there may be multiple beings involved, which likely required coordination... and that meant there was something organising them...

Kamari became aware at that moment of a strange wetness on his arm. He let out a long, slow breath, then opened his eyes and looked down. He was shocked to see that his right forearm was red-raw and bleeding, and the fingertips of his left hand were slick with blood. He only realised then that he had been subconsciously scratching all this time and with a jolt it hit him – that was where he had seen the black nodules on Mara...

Kamari had never admitted this to anyone, but he had a dread fear of sickness. For him it was the worst kind of foe – an unseen enemy that can steal in and take your life, no matter how strong or well-prepared you are. Kamari had seen this happen first-hand and it had scarred him deeply.

Back when Kamari was only five summers old, Tetsuo Shimura – an uncle on his mother's side – had come to live with them for a time in Aigano. He had been a blacksmith, big and tough as they come. After spending hours and hours every day beating bits of metal into shape, he had arms the size of tree trunks and used to make Kamari laugh by picking him up one handed, as though he weighed no more than a feather.

Tetsuo would often enter strong-man contests in his home village and would win them without fail. Kamari had always marvelled at his effortless strength and boundless charisma, and his unflappable, easy-going approach to life. At that age, he would look at his uncle and think that nothing could hurt him. How wrong he had been…

It was a few months after he arrived that Tetsuo began to feel unwell. It had started with muscle cramps and spasms, but soon he had difficulty breathing and became unable to get out of bed. Before long, his muscles began to waste away and that was what had terrified Kamari. His last image of his uncle had been of him lying on his bed, looking for all the world like a skeleton, so transformed that he could barely recognise him. It was seeing the man he admired brought down and realising how little his vast strength had helped him, that had left an indelible mark on Kamari.

Some enemies you just cannot see... his mind whispered.

True, but this one we can... he thought, picturing again the dark figure.

He looked down and noticed that he was reaching to scratch his arm again and managed to stop himself. This had happened throughout his life whenever he thought of sickness. It was like that feeling you get when someone mentions head lice and you can't help but scratch. At least, he hoped that was all it was...

He tried to pull himself together – it was time to head out and see to the dispensation of the rations. Ever since the blight had hit the rice crop, Kamari had enforced a rationing scheme to try and ensure they did not run out of food, but already their stocks had dropped worryingly low.

To avoid panic, he made sure the grain stores were kept locked at all times and had instructed Shio to organise guarding them. He had faith in his people, but could not shake the nagging concern that if it was discovered how low their stocks were running, then some villagers might take matters into their own hands to ensure the survival of their families...

In fact, there had already been a few close calls on that front. Two days ago, while the rations were being dispensed, a heated argument had broken out after one family claimed they had been given less than another. Kamari knew this to be false as he checked the sizes of each and every ration himself, but it had not been easy to calm the man down and convince him that everybody got the same.

He could not put it off any longer. He got to his feet and rolled down the sleeve of his kimono to hide his bleeding arm, for he knew that if Ellia saw it, she would worry. That reminded him that he should check on them once more before he headed out. Quietly, he tiptoed out of the main room and down the hall to the bedroom, where he carefully slid open the door and peeked inside.

The shutters on the window were closed, so it took a moment for his eyes to adjust to the dim light, but soon he could discern Ellia lying on a mat with Takashi and Meera asleep in her arms. He watched them silently for a moment and was just turning to leave when a voice stopped him.

'Shouldn't you be out seeing to the rations?' Ellia asked quietly. He turned back to face her.

'I'm just heading out now,' he replied in a whisper.

'How are they doing?' Ellia looked fondly at each of her peacefully slumbering babes.

'They're both fine,' she replied, kissing them gently on their foreheads. 'No signs of the sickness, but they have been a little upset – I think they miss seeing Mia.' Kamari felt a wrench of remorse and pity but knew this was for the best.

'It is safest for now if we continue to keep a distance from other people,' he said. 'I know it's hard for them, but...' Kamari's voice trailed off as the sound of raised voices reached his ears. Ellia looked up at him anxiously.

'What is it?' she whispered.

'I'm not sure...' Kamari replied. 'I'd better go – I'll be back as soon as I can...'

With that, Kamari turned and hurried off towards the front door, slipping on his sandals and darting outside in a heartbeat. As he hurried down the hill in the weak afternoon light, he looked sadly at the spot on the grass where Mia, Takashi and Meera used to play every day, now standing quiet and empty. He would see that space filled once more...

As he approached the village the voices grew louder and louder, their tone angry and frustrated.

What on earth has happened...? he wondered as he reached the bridge and crossed over into the main area of the village. He stopped a moment and listened – the voices seemed to be coming from the grain store where the rations were handed out. His heart sank.

Oh no...

Grimly, Kamari hurried towards the voices and rounded a building to discover a tense scene. The heads of most of the families had gathered outside the grain store – at a respectable distance from one another – and were facing down Shio, who had his arms raised in a placatory manner. Behind him, Jito

– Shio's younger brother – was trying to repair the damaged latch on the grain store. It was clear that someone had broken it…

'What is going on here?' Kamari said loudly, causing a hush to descend as the crowd turned towards him. The silence lasted only a moment before voices were raised in indignation and panic.

'We are almost out of food!'

'Our families will starve!'

'Why did you not tell us?'

'What are we going to eat?'

'The Spirits are angry – we must leave this place!'

As the voices crowded his mind – clamouring for attention – Kamari strode over to Shio and whispered in his ear.

'What happened?'

Shio, his face white as a sheet, turned to glance at his brother who was busy fixing the latch.

'I tried to stop them…' Shio began. 'They were queueing up early to receive their rations when they began questioning how much food we had left. I told them we had enough to last, but they did not believe me and before I knew what was happening, Teiji and Uto Orono had pushed past me and broken the latch to see for themselves. Now they all know how little remains… I am so sorry, Kamari…' he finished, looking shamefaced. Kamari placed a hand on his shoulder.

'It's alright, Shio,' he said. 'I am sorry I put you in this position.' Kamari took a breath, then turned to face the crowd sternly.

'I know you are all scared, for yourselves and your families,' he began, 'but I will not tolerate vandalism and harassment. If you have a problem, you will come speak to me – is that clear?' He looked around the crowd and saw several heads nodding mutely. 'Good. Now… Yes, it is true that our supplies are running low, but as I said at the start of this crisis, I *know* that we will endure as long as we pull together and show a little patience, understanding and self-sacrifice. What I had planned to announce anyway was that I have sent out a number of our best people to nearby towns and ports to seek trades for food and medicine. I cannot give you an exact date they will return, but I have faith they will be back soon, and when they are you will see that we are not alone.'

Kamari fell silent for a moment as those last two words echoed in his mind.

'Because, in the end, that's what it all comes down to – isn't it?' he continued. 'We are *not* alone. We are a *community*. It is so tempting in these times of fear and strife to retreat into yourself or your family and forget the needs and feelings of others. But that cannot – it *must not* – happen now. It would only take one of you, just one, to break – to do something you would not normally do and steal what you feel you need to survive, but in doing so you are not only tarnishing your honour but hurting and destabilising our entire community. It is in these difficult times that – more than ever – we must not look inward but outward and think of the good of everyone, not only ourselves. I have seen you all do this before and I have faith you can do it again. So, please; show patience, show understanding, and be prepared to go a little hungry for now so that everyone is able to eat. I *promise you* we will get through this together and come out stronger on the other side.' Kamari turned to Shio. 'Now, let us hand out the rations for the day.'

Wordlessly, Shio handed him the first of the ration packs and, after a few moments of shared glances and the odd whispered exchange, the villagers formed a line to receive their rations. For the next few minutes Kamari gave out rations to the reaching hands of his people like one in a trance, his mind reeling from what had almost happened.

They came so close... he thought. *So close already to collapse...*

And you can be sure this will not be the worst of it... his mind wheedled from the dark recesses. *These are but the first cracks to show...*

He snapped back to himself when he realised that the hands reaching out at that moment were those of Teiji and Uto Orono. The two brothers could not meet his eye and instead looked away shamefully, their arms held out for aid.

'We are sorry, Kamari,' they murmured in unison.

'It will not happen again,' Uto added. Kamari glared at them sternly a moment before replying.

'See that it doesn't,' he said at last. 'You are both better than that – act like it.'

'We will,' they guiltily chorused.

Kamari nodded as he handed them the rations and watched as they hurried back home.

I will need to keep an eye on them... he thought.

He turned back to the line to see a figure standing before him, hooded and cloaked. The man's head was downcast, his posture hunched, and Kamari realised he had no idea who it was. He tried to peer under the man's hood, but he did not raise his eyes.

'Uh, hello...?' Kamari began slowly. 'Who are you?'

The man did not respond, but Kamari realised that he was swaying on the spot, like one who has drunk too much rice wine. A low gurgle began to emanate from under the hood and Kamari started to feel uneasy.

'Look,' he said. 'I have a lot of people to get through, so either remove your hood and take your ration or go home and lie down – your choice.'

The man's breath rasped harshly and his body spasmed with a crunch of bones shifting. Kamari's hand went unconsciously to his sword hilt.

'Who are you...?' he whispered again.

Slowly the man raised his head and what Kamari saw made his blood run cold. It was Akai, but – like the ox before him – where his eyes should have been there was nothing but two holes of impenetrable, shifting shadow, set in a face contorted by pain and confusion. Kamari could almost taste his fear and distress, but it was clear some other force was controlling him. Slowly, Akai's hand went to an object hidden under his cloak.

'Akai…' Kamari breathed. 'Don't…'

But, before he could finish his sentence, Akai had drawn a katana and launched himself at Kamari with a guttural scream and in an instant, all hell broke loose. As Akai bore Kamari to the ground, several villagers yelled in shock and dashed for cover, while the rest staggered back in surprise.

Pinned to the grass, Kamari was stunned at the brute strength of the older man. With one hand he had gripped Kamari's wrists with a hold like iron, while the other hand brought his sword to bear on Kamari's throat. Kamari thrashed around like a landed fish, but try as he might, he could not wriggle free. He could just feel the sword point pricking his windpipe when Shio and Jito intervened, blindly swinging bits of timber that Akai effortlessly deflected – but it was enough of a distraction.

With a mighty effort, Kamari head-butted Akai full in the face and felt his opponent's nose break. Akai toppled sideways and Kamari was able to get to his feet, only for Akai to lash out with his blade and score a shallow cut along Kamari's stomach.

Clutching at the wound and with his sword in hand, Kamari took a step closer, vaguely aware that most of the villagers had now fled the area. Wildly, his opponent took another swing at him and Kamari dodged to one side, kicking him full in the chest and sending him hurtling backwards, but not all of him…

For a split second something remained where Akai had stood. A dark shape like a shadow given form lingered in the air. As Kamari watched horror-stricken, the shadow turned, it looked at him, then it melded back with Akai as he hit the floor.

For a moment Kamari stood frozen in uncomprehending horror, but Akai was not done yet. He staggered to his feet, his weapon held ready.

'Akai, don't do this…' Kamari said, holding up his hands soothingly. 'You are not yourself; we can fix this!'

Akai stared at him with his pitch-black eyes, oblivious to the group of armed villagers that had just appeared behind him. They had heard what Kamari said and were now whispering Akai's name.

'I can help you,' Kamari continued. 'Let me help you!'

Pain and fear washed over Akai's face like a wave, but they could not hold him back. With a strangled cry, he hurled himself at Kamari once more – sword held high – and as he brought it scything down, Kamari ducked out of the way and grimly, reluctantly, punched his own blade through Akai's chest.

In an instant Akai went limp and Kamari caught him, lowering him gently to the ground, his hood covering his face. A hysterical scream split the air as Akai's wife rushed over and threw herself to the ground beside him, weeping brokenly and calling his name in anguish. She moved to draw back his hood and for a moment Kamari wanted to stop her, but as she pulled it from his face Kamari saw with a shock that his eyes were back to normal, now staring sightlessly at the evening sky.

What on earth...? Kamari thought in fearful bewilderment.

He looked up past the gathering crowd and a shape caught his eye. The dark figure he had seen detach from Akai was standing at the rear of the crowd, silent and unseen. His suspicions were correct, it looked different to the other – there were certainly multiple beings involved. The figure locked eyes with him and he could feel its hatred and malevolence, then it turned and hurried over the bridge and up the western valley slope towards Dengai forest.

That is where the other one went... Kamari realised.

He felt a presence beside him and turned to see Shio standing there.

'Are you alright?' Shio murmured. Kamari waved this away.

'Yes, I'm fine but, did you... did you see anything... during the fight...?'

Shio looked at him oddly.

'Anything like... what...?' he replied.

'You didn't... you didn't see a dark...' Kamari stopped himself. Perhaps it was better this way. If anyone else had seen what he saw, it would only spread further panic.

A gasp went up from the crowd and Kamari looked over to see that they had found the black nodules on Akai's skin.

So that is how these creatures pass their sickness to the living, Kamari realised, thinking too of the ox. *That is how they have been helping it spread...*

The reaction from the crowd was instantaneous as many in the group covered their mouths and scurried away from the body.

It's getting worse, Kamari thought. *I have to find the source of this sickness. I have to find out what is orchestrating this and stop it, or it will tear our village apart...*

CHAPTER SEVEN

Night had fallen and a pale moon hung in a star-strewn sky, obscured by drifting cloudbanks that cast deeper shadows over the darkened earth. A chill breeze buffeted them gently as Takashi, Meera, Jaroe, Hina and Kaito approached the fringes of Dengai Forest in the weak moonlight. From where they were, the forest made a forbidding sight – the trees and the impenetrable darkness between them forming a barrier that seemed to say, '*Keep out!*'

With a wary look at Hina, Meera turned to Jaroe.

'How will we find a doorway to Sen'i?' she asked quietly. Jaroe looked up at the moon for a moment before responding.

'Doorways only open during the Spirit Hour,' he replied, turning to Meera. 'For that is when the walls between our two worlds are weakest and the spirits can walk freely between them. While there are doorways across the land, it is said that the heart of Sen'i resides somewhere in Dengai, so it is the most likely place to find the Senzo.'

'What do the doorways look like?' Takashi asked. 'How will we know one when we see it?'

Here, Kaito stepped forward excitedly.

'I can find one!' he said enthusiastically. 'I couldn't explain it at the time, but I had the urge to look into Sen'i and spent the last few months researching it – now I know why!' He turned to Jaroe.

'I can go ahead,' he continued eagerly. 'I will find one – I know what to look for!'

Jaroe stared at him critically. It bothered him that he could not read this over-excitable young wolf. Ever since Kaito first arrived, it seemed like wherever Jaroe looked, there he was, and – without fail – he would always have something to say. It seemed clear to him that Kaito was trying to prove something or get on his good side; but it was his motivations that Jaroe was uncertain of and this uncertainty worried him. He realised in that moment that he had been feeling off ever since the battle with Kichibei's forces at Harakima. But they had won that fight – why should it have affected him so...?

He blinked and shook his head as he came to his decision.

Fine... if the young fool wants to get himself lost amongst the trees then it's no skin off my nose, he thought.

'Alright, go on ahead,' Jaroe replied at last with a dismissive nod.

'I won't let you down!' Kaito said happily as he turned and hurried off into the forest, disappearing amongst the trees.

'Will he be alright on his own?' Meera asked.

'When he gives up, I'm sure he'll find his way back to us,' Jaroe replied indifferently. 'Let's continue on.'

With Jaroe in the lead, they approached the forest and entered the trees. Takashi looked up as they crossed the threshold, watching as the moon and stars abruptly vanished behind the high leafy canopy like a blanket being drawn over them. Then, they were in.

The first thing he noticed was the utter silence and stillness of the forest. Not a breath of wind seemed to reach them as they strode along and for a time no one spoke.

In the stifling quiet, Takashi felt his mind begin to wander and it returned to a thought that had plagued him ever since they left the quarry.

What had Kenjin meant when he said: "One thing should never become two"?

It was a proverb he had never heard before, but it had sounded like he was talking about him and Meera – so what did he mean by "one thing"? Takashi was just turning to ask Meera about it when a voice cut across him.

'Hey, over here! I've found one!' It was Kaito, and at his voice they all turned to look in surprise, but their surprise was unmatched by that of Jaroe.

He actually found one? he thought in disbelief. *Normally only a trained eye can spot them…*

Together, they hurried over to him with Jaroe following dubiously at the rear. On reaching Kaito, they all looked around expectantly, but at first glance there was nothing immediately obvious to see.

'So… where is it?' Hina asked brusquely.

'Right there,' Kaito replied, indicating the base of an unremarkable rocky outcrop.

Hina stared hard at the spot for a moment.

'There's nothing there,' she said at last in annoyance. 'It's just a…'

'He's right,' Jaroe cut across her as he stared fixedly at the spot. 'Look closer Hina, it does not want to be found so is not visible from all angles, but it is there…'

Looking sceptical, Hina moved to one side and soon her eyes widened in surprise.

'I… I see it…' she breathed.

With a glance at each other, Takashi and Meera moved to stand beside her and soon they could both see it too. Jaroe was right, it was almost invisible from most angles, but from where they stood, they could just about see it. It was like looking at the slim gap between two curtains blown in the breeze; a wavering, flickering line of light that hung suspended in the air before them.

'It is just like my research said,' Kaito said quietly. 'Shall we go inside?' He took a step forward, but Jaroe stopped him with a look.

'I will go first,' he said firmly. 'But, before we enter, remember – most spirits will tolerate us, but many feel nothing but envy for the living. So, do not forget Kenjin's words: stay together, move fast, and most important of all, do not forget our purpose – we do not want any of us losing ourselves in there.'

With that, Jaroe turned, took a breath, and passed through the doorway without another word. Kaito's eyes were bright as he watched him go. He leapt over to the doorway but stopped before passing through.

'See you on the other side!' he said, then bounded forward and vanished.

Hina was up next and moved purposefully towards the door, passing through without a pause or a sound, leaving Takashi and Meera standing side by side.

Meera looked doubtfully at the door for a moment.

'Don't worry,' Takashi murmured. 'I'm right here with you.'

Meera nodded and walked cautiously over to the door, pausing only a moment before she stepped through and disappeared, leaving Takashi alone.

As he stood there in the silence, Takashi felt the trees draw in closer around him. He took a breath to steady himself, then stepped up to the ribbon of light through which he could now see vague, indistinct shapes. Bracing himself, he moved forwards and his head breached the doorway.

Passing through was like nothing he had ever experienced before. The closest thing he could liken it to was walking under a waterfall. He felt a weight pressing down upon him and his vision rippled as he was gripped by an intense cold that knocked the breath from his body. For a moment he felt like he could not breathe and panic gripped him. The light seemed brighter ahead and he dashed desperately towards it, feeling his lungs tighten and his chest constrict.

He could barely see, could hardly breathe; his vision began to darken, then, like breaching the surface of a lake, he was through, gasping for breath on the other side. He looked up blearily to see the others standing around him, panting.

'Well, that was fairly unpleasant,' Kaito said wryly.

'No one said coming to the spirit realm was going to be easy,' Jaroe muttered.

As Takashi's breathing returned to normal, his vision slowly cleared and he – alongside his companions – was able to take his first proper look at Sen'i. What he saw took his breath away.

At first glance, Sen'i looked much like their own world and it was clear they were still in some version of Dengai Forest, but it was like he was viewing it through a heat haze. Everywhere he looked the landscape seemed to shimmer and eddy, its colours soft and muted like a watercolour painting, spreading and blending into each other like dye bleeding out of a garment in the wash. Takashi had to strain his eyes to see where one tree ended and another began and if he relaxed his gaze, it was like everything became one, homogenous whole.

'The accounts I read did not do it justice...' Kaito breathed in awe.

As he stood there drinking-in his surroundings, Takashi felt strangely at peace. He could feel the connections all around him drawing everything together, binding them tight – human or animal, plant or mineral – in this place everything was one, everything was equal.

'It is beautiful…' Meera whispered.

'It is beautiful to the living,' Jaroe murmured, 'but to the Pilgrims it is a reminder of what they are leaving behind, of the connections they may have missed.'

'The Pilgrims?' Takashi asked.

Jaroe shot him a brief look before replying – clearly, he had not yet forgiven him.

'Sen'i is a… it is a transitional space,' he began slowly, 'a place where all spirits go, both human and animal, before their essence leaves this world completely. For many it is a second chance, an opportunity to say their last goodbyes if they were snatched away too quickly, but eventually all feel the pull of the Pilgrimage – a final journey that will guide them to the Senzo and away from this place forever.'

Jaroe took a step away from them and reached out to one of the nearby trees, which rippled under his touch.

'There are several types of spirit in Sen'i,' he continued. 'The Pilgrims are the spirits who pass through. Most do not linger and continue quickly along the Pilgrimage, but some… some cannot let go and remain behind, ignoring the pull of the Pilgrimage for a chance to stay close to their loved ones. That is why there are the Shepherds. It is their job to find the Lost and guide them back towards the path. Most go willingly when asked, but some refuse to ever follow and become the Fallen – bitter and twisted spirits that have forgotten who they are. It is for this reason they have the Guardians – spirits deemed worthy enough to guard this realm from the Fallen and all else who would do it harm.'

'So, what happens on this Pilgrimage?' Meera asked, looking around her in wonderment.

'Little is known of the Pilgrimage itself,' Jaroe replied, 'for normally, none return from it. But I have an idea where it might start and if the Senzo is anywhere, it is somewhere along there. So, follow me, and remember – quick and quiet – we are unwanted guests here…'

With that, Jaroe set off northward and the rest of the group followed, still looking around them in amazement. At the rear of the group, Takashi walked with his head down, feeling with every step he took the life pulsing through the earth and seeing the effects of his passage ripple out around him like water. It was hypnotic, transfixing, but it made him realise all the more keenly that even here, and even with Meera so close by, the guiding feeling had not yet returned and, when Meera looked back at him – eyes alight with wonder – he discovered that he was still unable to intuit the emotions of another wolf. Feeling these connections all around only made him realise how isolated he felt in that moment.

What has happened to me…? he wondered again despairingly. *How do I fix this…?*

He was so wrapped up in his thoughts that he almost walked into Kaito, who had stopped dead in front of him. Takashi was about to protest when Kaito spoke.

'Look,' he breathed.

Takashi followed his gaze and caught his first sighting of a spirit in Sen'i. As far back as he could remember, Takashi had always wanted to see a spirit. Since leaving Aigano after the barbarian attack, he had seen what he believed to be spirits, but he had never seen one like this. This was how he had always pictured it – a spirit unaware of his presence that would go about its business.

It was a rabbit spirit and it was sitting in the grass ahead with its back to them. Its outline was frail and wispy, like smoke caught on the wind, and it emanated a pale, moon-like glow. When it moved, it did so slowly, cautiously; clearly lost and confused by its surroundings.

'It has not long arrived,' Jaroe said under his breath. 'It does not yet understand…'

Takashi looked at it sadly and wondered how it had died – hopefully it had been quick and painless. He was just saying a prayer for its swift passage along the Pilgrimage when something caught his eye. Another rabbit spirit had darted into view, catching the attention of the first. The newcomer was running full tilt – ears back in fear – and within seconds, the first rabbit had caught its distress and fled alongside it.

'What are they…?' Meera began to ask, but she got no further as a deer spirit bounded across their path, followed swiftly by two others. Jaroe sniffed the air, tense and alert.

'Something's wrong…' he whispered. 'Follow me.'

Silent as ghosts, the group padded off north-east in the direction the spirits had fled from. As they walked, the trees became closer together, cutting off sightlines and forcing them to weave their way between the massive, gnarled trunks.

'I wonder what frightened them…?' Kaito whispered. 'Could it have been a Fallen? Or is there…'

'Quiet!' Jaroe cut across him. 'I hear something…'

They stopped still and listened, and sure enough, a high-pitched keening wail – like something in pain – could be heard coming from up ahead. Jaroe turned to the group.

'Meera, stay at the back,' he instructed. 'The rest of you stick close behind me.'

With Jaroe in the lead, they slowly advanced towards the sound – hearing the distress in the cry intensify with every step they took. A few paces behind Kaito, Takashi glanced back to check on Meera and could see that she was upset.

'Are you alright?' he whispered.

'It is unbearable…' she gasped. 'It is in so much pain…'

A massive cedar tree reared in front of them and as they rounded its great, twisted trunk, they discovered the source of the noise.

It was a fox spirit. The poor creature was lying at the base of the tree, writhing in agony – a ball of pain and misery. Its glow was faint, weakening; Takashi was sure he could see it fading with every second. The spirit seemed oblivious to their presence, consumed by its anguish, its light growing dimmer and dimmer until finally it went out and the spirit lay still.

Jaroe took a step closer and sniffed it.

'Something is not right…' he muttered.

'What do you think…?' Kaito began, but he got no further as the spirit suddenly jerked to its feet with a screech and scrabbled out of sight behind the tree. A terrible hissing gurgle reached their ears and they looked at each other in shock.

'We should move on…' Meera whispered. 'Now…'

But it was too late for that. From around the base of the tree the fox spirit re-emerged slowly, malevolently, but it was changed… Gone was its luminescent glow – its whole being now exuding darkness like a fog. Gone too was its graceful form, replaced with a twisted mockery of life – two sharp, pointed heads, riddled with jagged teeth, fur black and glistening like flayed skin, and seven writhing, whip-like tails that scythed the air in anticipation. Its empty, black eyes were set upon them, its twin maws open in savage snarls as it advanced with a relentless intensity.

'What is wrong with it…?' Kaito breathed, aghast.

The spirit was no more than a few paces from them when it lunged and Hina was the first to react. She leapt at it with a snarl and bulled it to one side. It landed with a thud in the dirt and instantly flipped back on its feet, hissing fiercely. With a quick glance at Meera that said, '*Stay where you are*', Takashi darted after Hina.

Jaroe was tensed and ready to pounce, but before he did so, he looked across at Kaito. He had expected to see him trembling in fear at the prospect of a real fight, but was surprised to see the young wolf standing ready like a coiled spring – a snarl on his lips – and before even Jaroe could act, he had leapt into the fray with the others.

With a howl, Jaroe bounded in after him and joined the fight. The fox spirit was now surrounded but was making vicious, lightning-swift attacks at any who came close. Takashi tried to circle around it, but its whip-sharp tails lashed out, scoring several cuts down his flank. During this momentary distraction, Kaito made a lunge, but the fox spirit sprang at him, bowling him over and breaking out of their circle in the same instant.

No longer surrounded, the fox spirit saw Meera standing alone and rushed her. With a banshee-like shriek, it pounced and bore her to the ground. Pinned to the floor and weakened as she was, Meera was hard pressed to keep the spirit's snapping jaws away from her as it ferociously sought to tear out her throat. It was now so close, she could see straight into the gaping voids of its eyes – could feel herself falling into their darkness – when suddenly, the spirit was yanked hissing from her.

Hina had grabbed one of its tails in her jaws and hurled it into a nearby tree, where it collided heavily and slid to the floor. Takashi hurried over to check on Meera.

'Are you...?' he began.

'I'm fine,' she replied breathlessly. 'Go!'

Takashi nodded and leapt back after the spirit. It was now standing at the base of the tree faced down by Jaroe, Hina and Kaito. It crouched low, poised to spring, but instead did something they were not expecting and turned. With incredible agility, the spirit bounded a few paces up the tree, then sprang from it – up and over the others – and launched itself at the approaching Takashi.

It happened so quickly that he was caught completely by surprise. Before he knew it, Takashi was tumbling in the dirt with the spirit, narrowly avoiding its jaws and the lethal swipes of its tails. They came to a stop with the spirit on top of him and Takashi desperately looked for an opening to end this. But its strength seemed boundless and, try as he might, he could neither find an opening nor break free.

He raked at the spirit with his back legs, but it was no use... Its jaws were sinking ever-closer to his throat, when suddenly – with a yelp of pain and surprise – one of its heads went limp. Looking up, Takashi saw Hina with her jaws around its neck and the shock of what had happened distracted the spirit long enough for Takashi to wrap his teeth around its other neck, and bite down...

The spirit went limp in an instant and the fog that surrounded it faded away. Its outline shimmered like light on waves, then it slowly shrank into the ground and was gone. The others gathered around Takashi and Hina and stared at the spot it had been in shock and bewilderment.

'That cannot have been a Fallen…' Kaito whispered. 'It is nothing like my research said…'

'That was no Fallen,' Jaroe confirmed as he glanced warily around them.

'It looked… sick…' Hina said quietly.

'Whatever was wrong with it, one thing is abundantly clear,' Jaroe began, 'we must complete our mission fast and get out of here. Let's move – there may be more of them around…'

With that, he turned and set off northwards once more, Kaito close on his heels. Takashi turned to Meera.

'Did it hurt you?' he asked anxiously.

Meera looked up at him wearily.

'No, I'm alright,' she replied. 'It just knocked the wind out of me.'

Takashi nodded in relief, then turned to follow after Jaroe and Kaito, leaving Meera and Hina alone. Hina turned to her.

'So, too weak to bear the gift and too weak to even defend yourself,' she said scathingly. 'How were you ever considered worthy?'

With a derisive sneer, she followed after the others, leaving Meera once more on her own, Hina's last words echoing in her mind.

I don't know… Meera thought brokenly. *I don't know why I was chosen…*

Head bowed in shame and confusion, she followed after the others.

Near the head of the group, Takashi and Kaito were walking side by side and Kaito could see that his companion was thinking deeply.

'You're wondering how we were able to touch the spirit,' he said, as though he had read his mind. Takashi looked at him in surprise.

'How... how did you know that?'

'Because I have been wondering the same thing myself,' he replied. 'My research indicated it was possible, but not why...'

A few paces ahead of them, Jaroe replied without looking back.

'Your books and scrolls cannot tell you everything,' he said gruffly, 'but I can tell you this much. Like the spirits, we wolves are transitory creatures, stuck between two worlds. We have already lived our lives – these bodies are but temporary vessels enabling us to continue our duties. In many ways, we share the same plane of existence as the spirits – that is why we can touch them, and that is why we are in grave danger if we linger here too long...'

Takashi's spirits sank at the reminder in these words.

If these bodies were indeed only gifted so we could continue our duties... he thought, *then perhaps Meera and I were never meant to be...*

He looked back to see her following slowly at the rear of the group, head down.

She looks so tired... he thought. *I have to help her... As long as she survives this, as long as she is safe... whatever happens to me after... I do not care...*

They were just rounding a large rocky outcrop when a sight met their eyes that stopped them in their tracks.

'This cannot be unrelated...' Jaroe breathed. 'There is something terribly wrong here...'

As Meera and Hina joined them, they beheld the sight together. What they saw they could not explain, but for some reason this part of the forest looked... wrong... diseased...

It was as though all the colour had leached out of the area, leaving nothing but shades of black and grey behind. The edges of objects, that had once been blurred and indistinct, were now sharply, jaggedly in focus – as though they had shut themselves off from one another. Where before Takashi had felt connections all around him, here he felt... nothing... nothing at all... but his body was pervaded by a clawing, biting cold that drove deep into his marrow.

Teeth chattering, Takashi turned to the group.

'Do you feel that cold?' he asked. 'What has happened here...?'

'I have no idea...' Jaroe replied quietly. 'I have never seen anything like it before.'

'Maybe we should go around it?' Hina said. They all turned to look left and right, only to find that it stretched out of sight in both directions.

'We cannot waste time going around,' Jaroe said determinedly. 'Our path leads us through it, and that is the way we will go…'

Without another word, he stepped closer to the darkened area, but stopped on the threshold and hesitated. After a long pause he slowly, tentatively, lowered his leg and stepped inside. He held a second, then took another step, and another, and another.

'I think… I think it is alright,' he said. 'Come, follow me.'

Nervously, the group followed after him into the darkness and felt the cold descend on them like a lead weight. They huddled together as they moved to try and retain heat, but it made no difference, and before long they were all shivering uncontrollably.

'I… I do not like this,' Kaito mumbled. 'This place… I can feel nothing… How much further is it…?'

Shakily, Jaroe raised his head to check.

'If… if what I was told is true, then… then it cannot be too far now,' he replied with difficulty.

A sound away to their left made Meera jerk her head around.

'Did anyone hear that…?' she whispered.

'I heard it…' Hina replied. 'There is something out there…'

'Then let us not wait to meet it,' Jaroe said, breaking into a run in the same breath. The others followed suit and soon they were sprinting full pelt through the cloying darkness as more and more sounds began to ring out from the trees surrounding them.

'They're all around us!' Kaito hissed.

Glancing about, Takashi swore he could see eyes looking out at him from amongst the trees – eyes like deep wells in the shadow.

'There's light ahead!' Hina yelled and, looking up, Takashi could see it too. Hearts racing, they dug deep and powered forwards as the light grew closer and closer. Heavy footsteps could now clearly be heard on both sides as whatever it was closed in.

'Almost there! Almost there!' Kaito repeated as they thundered on – lungs fit to burst – and just when they felt they could run no more, they finally broke out of the darkness and back into the light.

They skidded to a stop and turned back to see... nothing...

As suddenly as it had started, it was over, and there was not a sound to be heard anywhere.

'What... what was that...?' Meera asked breathlessly.

'Something you were lucky to have survived...' a voice said.

As one, they whirled around to discover a sight they could not believe they had missed. Standing before them was a huge torii – an ornate gateway over twenty feet tall, its twin circular pillars made of crimson-painted cedar and its dual, upward curving lintels painted too in crimson and black. A well-worn path led north from the gate, disappearing off into the distance to some unknown destination. Relief flooded Takashi as he stared at it – torii were only ever used to mark the entrance to a sacred place. They had found the start of the Pilgrimage, but the source of the voice was nowhere in sight…

'Who's there?' Jaroe called into the tense silence. 'Show yourself!'

For a moment nothing happened, then a figure stepped out from behind one of the pillars and turned slowly to face them. It was a man, but from his wispy outline and pale luminescence, it was clear he was a spirit – the first human spirit Takashi had ever seen. He was dressed in the garb of a monk, including layered kimonos – yellow on white – and a wide, domed straw hat that hid most of his face. He was short and a little stocky, but bore himself with the utmost ease and self-assurance as he approached them lightly over the fallen leaves.

'My name is Reo,' the spirit said as he stopped a few paces from them. 'I am a Guardian of Sen'i. I must say, we have not seen any wolves here for a considerable time…'

'Believe me, we wouldn't have come if it were not of the utmost importance,' Jaroe replied, a hint of reverence in his tone. 'But our purpose can wait – can you tell us what is going on? What has happened to the spirits and the forest?'

Reo looked back the way they had come at the darkened area.

'We do not yet fully understand it,' he began. 'But we know this much… A sickness is spreading throughout Sen'i…'

'A sickness…?' Kaito echoed.

'How it is being transmitted is a mystery, but it is ancient,' Reo continued, 'ancient and powerful. It is killing the forest and any spirit it infects becomes enraged and twisted, driven by pain and confusion to do terrible things. There are not many Guardians left and we are hard-pressed to hold them back – our only hope now is the Senzo…'

'The Senzo is why we are here,' Hina said quietly.

'We seek the Senzo to discuss a grave matter,' Jaroe added.

'He has gone to seek the source of this sickness,' Reo said, looking off north through the gate. 'If you follow the Pilgrimage, you may find him somewhere along it, but whether he will have time to listen to your request, I do not know…'

'We have to try,' Jaroe said. 'And if we find him, we will offer what help we can.'

'Then you have my blessing and my thanks,' Reo said, taking a few steps back and waving them towards the gate. 'Time is of the essence and I must return to my patrol – I wish you luck.'

With Jaroe in the lead, the group set off towards the gate, bowing their heads to Reo as they passed. At the back of the group, Meera slowed as she drew level with the Guardian.

'Has anyone ever returned from the Pilgrimage?' she asked, in barely more than a whisper. Reo gave her a sideways look.

'They have,' he replied after a moment. 'If the Senzo willed it.'

With that, he turned and headed out on his patrol. With her mind abuzz, Meera followed after the others and set off along the Pilgrimage.

CHAPTER EIGHT

Myriad stars danced on the water's surface as the shadows of fish wove between them, for all the world like they were afraid of their brilliant glow. Kamari watched them unseeingly as he gazed into the Daku River from the bridge at the centre of Aigano, his thoughts afire with worry.

Since Akai's death the previous night, tensions in the village had skyrocketed. No one was leaving their homes for any reason and many had taken to guarding their front doors – every person now looking upon their neighbours with outright fear and mistrust. The only positive was that no one had mentioned seeing the dark figure – Kamari could only imagine the chaos if they had.

But worse than all that was the news that morning of the first sickness-related death in the village. Tayo – the boy Kamari had seen collapse in the rice paddy and the first known human case of the sickness – had finally succumbed. He had always been a little weak and scrawny and had well-known breathing difficulties that the sickness had clearly preyed upon. His parents were inconsolable, and where normally the whole village would have rallied around the grieving family, there was instead only suspicion and alienation.

Reflecting on the crisis thus far, it saddened Kamari that his people had reacted the way they had. He had hoped that – as with Kichibei – they would have faced this new crisis with fierce wills and strong spirits, but instead they seemed to be coming apart at the seams.

But this is different to Kichibei, his subconscious reminded him. *This is an enemy they have no power over – this is far more insidious than the actions of mortal men...*

It was true. In his heart he could not blame them, but this unrest did not make the situation any easier. He gripped the hilt of the sword at his side as he turned west to look at Dengai Forest. He had to find the source. He had to put a stop to this... and if that meant going to battle once more, then so be it...

After the encounter with Kichibei's army, Kamari had hoped with all his heart never to see combat again, but so far this sickness had forced him to take two lives. He had seen so much death already for one so young, and that particular conflict would always live in a dark place in his mind.

It had all started when, after years of patiently waiting, Lord Shigako Kichibei was finally given an opening to attack when the battle with Zian Agran left Lord Orran's Kurai army dreadfully diminished. He had set out immediately with his forces, intent upon reclaiming the domain he believed was rightfully his – a domain his ancestors had lost to the Orran line generations ago.

Thankfully, Lord Orran had received word of their plans and sent Takashi to find the wolves and beg for their aid, which – after first helping them with a crisis of their own – he had. With the wolves by their side, the battle with Kichibei was fought and won, but at a high price. In his efforts to cut the head off the snake, Takashi lost his life at the hands of Kichibei, but not before he and Meera were able to put an end to their foe, once and for all.

The battle had taken its toll on Kamari, both mentally and physically. Losing his friend had felt like losing a piece of himself and he had grieved for days after. But soon he had come to realise that Takashi was exactly where he wanted to be, and death had simply been the next step on his path to Meera. But, as happy as that thought made him, it did not stop him missing his friend.

It was this fear of loss that made him never want to see another battle. But, as things stood, if he did not go to battle once more, there was a chance that he, and everyone else in Aigano, could lose everything – and he could not let that happen.

He straightened and took a breath when a voice rang out from the darkness.

'I know that look…'

Kamari peered into the shadows as a figure stepped onto the bridge beside him. It was Ellia.

'Tell me what is going on.'

Kamari stared at her a moment in the moonlight, his eyes tracing every familiar, beloved facet of her face, committing it to memory.

'I… I have to go…' he said eventually.

'Go?' she echoed after a pause. 'Go where?'

'To find the source,' he replied. 'The source of this sickness – it is the only way to end it.'

'What… what makes you think there is a source…?' she asked in bewilderment. 'It is a sickness, not a…'

'This is no normal sickness…' he replied. 'It is directed… it is… targeted… it is… unnatural…'

Ellia gave him a perplexed look.

'What do you mean… unnatural…?' she asked falteringly.

Kamari sighed and turned away from her. He had wanted to protect her from this, but he could hide it no longer. She had a right to know. She deserved to know why he was leaving.

'I saw what it is that started this… what is helping it spread…' he answered in a barely audible whisper. 'They are monsters… spirits… demons… I do not know what… But I know what they can do. I have seen them walk our village at night. I have seen them leave the houses of the infected. I have seen them possess the living, leaving sickness in their wake…'

'Akai…?' Ellia breathed, wide-eyed with fear. Kamari nodded.

'And I have seen where they run to after every visit…' he continued, pointing off towards Dengai

Forest. Ellia glanced over her shoulder, then turned back to him.

'No medicine in the world could help us now,' he said, taking her face in his hands. 'Our only hope is if I track one of these things to its origin, find out what is driving them, and put a stop to it – one way or another – before there are any more deaths...'

Ellia gazed searchingly into his face but said nothing.

'There is no other way – I must do this...' he whispered fervently.

He could see the tears forming in her eyes as she stared into his, but they did not fall. Finally, she blinked and brushed down his kimono busily.

'Well, of course you must,' she said at last in her usual business-like tone. 'I cannot believe you have not already left! But... what about your fear...?'

'My... my fear...?' Kamari replied uncertainly.

She put her hands on her hips and gave him her most withering look.

'You cannot hide things from me, Kamari Shiro,' she said. 'Did you think I hadn't noticed that you're terrified of sickness?'

Kamari gaped at her.

'I... I thought... I didn't know you...' he stammered.

'If that was your attempt at hiding something, then at least I know you're not cheating on me!' she said. 'You practically yelled it from the rooftops – did you think I didn't notice you run a mile every time the children caught a sniffle? I am surprised you managed to keep these demons from me for so long!'

Her voice softened as she straightened his kimono.

'Will you be alright?'

Images of the black nodules, Akai's twisted face and the eyes of the ox suddenly filled his thoughts. He felt the familiar itch on his arm but fought the urge to scratch it.

'I'll be fine,' he replied, more confidently than he felt. 'I have to be.'

She gripped his arm and pulled him close, kissing him passionately on the lips, then stepped aside to let him pass.

'Then what are you waiting for?' she said. 'Get going!'

He could not keep the smile from spreading across his face as he looked at her.

'I love you,' he said.

'I know,' she replied. 'Now get moving! Shoo!'

He hesitated only a moment, then hurried past her, calling over his shoulder.

'Be safe and keep the children out of trouble!'

Here she stomped her foot in mock indignation.

'Aww, but we were going to sharpen your swords and play with the fishhooks!'

Kamari's smile grew wider still as he hurried onwards.

Gods, I love her... he thought.

He had already packed a small bag in preparation for his departure, but he could not leave without a quick stop first. He sprinted up the wooden steps of his house, eased open the front door, then moved as quietly as he could to the bedroom. He peeked around the half-open door and there they were – both sound asleep on the mat.

As he stared at the peaceful, sleeping faces of his children, he knew that he would do anything to protect them – even face his greatest fear.

'I love you, my darlings,' he whispered, then he turned and moved swiftly to the back door and out into the night. A chill wind was blowing as he stood on the veranda and looked up the steep valley side towards Dengai Forest. He squared his shoulders then set off north-west up the slope to intersect with the path he had seen the dark figures take.

It had rained a lot the previous night and the ground was slippery underfoot, making the going tough. Every now and then Kamari would stumble and slide, and soon he was caked in mud and sweating profusely.

It has been a long time since I last did this... he thought with a smile.

When he and Takashi had been young, they had often played out here; climbing trees like monkeys, wriggling into fox dens, sliding down hills and generally getting into mischief before coming back home filthy and bedraggled to receive a reprimand from their parents. But it had always been worth it – every single time.

This reminded Kamari that he had never been to the top of the valley before. Their parents had always told them not to venture too deep into Dengai

Forest. There were stories of children going missing there and it was said to be a domain of the spirits. Of course, being young, they had often ventured *close* to the top of the valley – just enough to feel daring and rebellious without ever actually breaking their parents' command – but already, he realised, he was past the furthest point he had ever been.

Can't stop now… he thought ruefully.

Before long, he had joined the route the dark figures had taken and, after a quick glance east to confirm for sure, he turned west and began to scramble directly upwards to see where it was they had been going.

Finally, after a few painful falls and a lot of cursing, he made it to the top and turned to look out across the valley. It was only then that he realised just how high he had climbed and it was dizzying. Aigano sat far below him like a child's toy, the weak glow of candlelight in a few windows the only signs of life.

As he stared out across his home, a movement somewhere below caught his eye. At first, he thought it was a bird or a bat flitting past, but then he saw it again and something about the way it moved was odd… He strained his eyes in the darkness, scanning for any sign of it, and there it was again – a dark shape hurrying between the trees, heading his way.

It is one of them!

A moment of triumphant excitement gripped him, but it was gone in a flash as he realised what this meant – the creature had once more been spreading its sickness through Aigano… Kamari's face hardened as he watched it unwittingly approach, then he turned and cast around for a hiding spot. He noticed a large shrub near the base of a tree and hurried over to it, diving inside before turning to face the direction the figure was approaching from.

He did not have long to wait…

Like a living shadow, the creature drew near, and Kamari was surprised to discover that it made not a single sound as it moved through the fallen leaves. From his crouched position in the shrub he could see very little, so he shifted slightly to get a better angle and, to his horror, a twig snapped beneath him.

The creature instantly froze and its head whipped round to face his hiding place. For a moment it stood there – tense and alert – listening for any further sounds. Then it slowly began to prowl towards him. From where he was, Kamari could see very little of it; it was clearly humanoid, but the way it moved was unnatural, almost animalistic.

As it drew closer and closer, Kamari could see more of its lower half and he realised that its feet, although human, bore long, needle-sharp claws. Its skin was darkest black and glinted as though covered in a viscous fluid. But what really surprised him was that its outline appeared wispy and ethereal and a dark, fog-like substance seemed to cling to it.

What is this thing…? Kamari wondered horror-stricken.

The creature was almost upon him when it stopped and glanced up at the sky. It had clearly realised something, for it gave one last look at Kamari's hiding spot, then turned and hurried off the way it had been heading, west into the forest. Wasting no time, Kamari extricated himself from the bush and set off after it as quietly as possible.

In the night-darkened forest, Kamari was hard pressed to keep up, for the creature moved with incredible speed, darting from tree to tree so fast that on several occasions he almost lost it. At one point it vanished round the base of a large tree and when it finally came back in sight, Kamari had to skid to a stop, for it had halted on the edge of a clearing.

Peering around a tree, Kamari was finally afforded a clear view of it as it gazed up at the sky. He could not see its face, but it was indeed human and from its garb and hair style had the appearance of a masterless warrior. What was strange though was that – although a chill wind was blowing – its garments remained perfectly still.

So, it is a spirit... Kamari realised. *But it is no ordinary human spirit...*

As he stood there watching, the spirit glanced down at something unseen in the clearing, then quickly returned to looking up. Curiosity finally got the better of him as Kamari followed the spirit's gaze and looked up at the night sky. A three-quarter moon and a dazzling array of stars met his eyes – but nothing out of the ordinary.

He looked back and was shocked to see that the spirit had vanished. Throwing caution to the wind, he sprinted out into the clearing and cast around, but there was not a trace to be seen anywhere. He looked up at the sky once more and it occurred to him that it had just crossed over into the Spirit Hour. Desperately, he scoured the area, hurrying back and forth, when a blast of cold air on his arm stopped him dead.

Where had that come from...?

He turned slowly on the spot, holding out his hand before him like a blind man. A tingle of frosty air on his fingers directed his attention and he stared hard at the spot. At first, he saw nothing, then he became vaguely aware of a sliver of weak light hanging suspended at the centre of the clearing.

Not quite believing his eyes, he circled slowly around and as he did so, the strand of light widened, revealing shifting shapes beyond. He stepped closer, peering into it, and could discern what looked like a forest, similar to where he now stood, but different... other...

Tentatively, he held out a hand to the light and, after a moment's hesitation, thrust it inside. He had been braced for pain, but instead felt only cold. He withdrew his hand and stared hard at this otherworldly doorway.

There is nowhere else it could have gone... he thought. *I have to follow it...*

He stood back and closed his eyes, taking several deep breaths to steady himself for whatever lay ahead. As he searched for calm – for resolve – the images of the black nodules, Akai and the eyes of the ox broke through his concentration, but with great determination he forced them down again.

He gripped his sword handle tightly as he opened his eyes and faced the doorway, then, without further hesitation, he stepped forward and entered.

At once the temperature plummeted and the past hit him like boulder. As he was enveloped by freezing air, he found himself back – back walking the snowy pass between Morikai and Kirina, back in the snowstorm that had taken his parents' lives, back in the body of a scared boy fleeing from one danger to another.

As he passed slowly through the doorway, he could almost feel the weight of the snow all around him, feel its resistance with every step he took, feel his mother and father pressing in tightly around him, sharing what little warmth they had. Tears sprang to his eyes as the memories of his last journey with his parents overwhelmed him.

I miss you… he thought, grief welling up inside him. *I miss you so much…*

As they had that day, his eyes began to close against his will, and it was a struggle to keep them open as the fearsome cold did its work. He stumbled and almost fell but managed to stagger onwards. It was so difficult to move, the snow felt like it was up to his shoulders. He couldn't keep going… he had to stop, he had to rest, he had to…

At that moment he tripped and fell and as he hit the forest floor, the cold vanished and so too did the memories, leaving him numb and shaking in the fallen leaves. Breathlessly, he rolled onto his back and looked blearily behind where he could just about discern the ribbon of light that marked the doorway.

I'm through... he thought with relief. *I made it...*

He was just getting to his feet to survey the area around him when a tingling sensation down his spine made him pause, crouched – tense and alert. He was not alone... something was nearby... He scanned the forest ahead, ignoring for now its strange appearance, as he searched for any sign of movement.

Then he froze. Some innate, primal instinct, deep in his core, was screaming at him to turn around. It was an ingrained, animalistic sense, and he obeyed it at once. He whipped around, reaching for his sword in the same breath, and came face to face with the spirit.

He had thought it was human – and it had been once – but now you could barely tell. Its eyes were the whirling, black eyes of the ox and as it leered at him, its mouth gaped horrifyingly wide – a smile from ear to ear – displaying row upon row of deadly, dagger-like teeth.

Forgetting for a moment what he was facing, Kamari swung his sword at the spirit only for the blade to pass harmlessly through, causing the spirit's smile to widen still further. With its eyes locked on his, it took a step closer and Kamari realised at once that he could not hope to fight this creature.

Run, you idiot! his subconscious screamed.

Without a second thought he turned and sprinted away and, after watching him go for an amused moment, the spirit set off in pursuit.

As he ran, branches raked Kamari's face, but he paid them no heed as he pelted onwards, feeling rather than seeing the spirit gaining on him. Up ahead, the forest seemed to change, as though a deeper shadow hung over it, but Kamari could not avoid it and so charged inside, feeling once more the temperature plummet around him. But this time he did not let memories overtake him and instead focussed on putting one foot in front of the other as the spirit gradually closed the gap between them.

He had been so focussed on watching his footing that when he next glanced up, he was surprised to see a huge torii gate standing not too far ahead. Like everyone in Hirono, Kamari knew that torii were the entrances to sacred land...

If I can get there, I might be safe... he thought, as he raced onwards and the spirit drew closer and closer, its clawed hands reaching out towards him.

I'll be safe there... he thought. *It will not follow me... I'll be safe there... I'll be safe...*

CHAPTER NINE

The Pilgrimage stretched out before them – a rough, cobbled path that wove its way lazily into the distance. At the rear of the group, Takashi and Meera walked side by side in silence as they looked sorrowfully around them. The Pilgrimage had clearly once been beautiful – a fitting send-off for any spirit taking the journey – but the sickness had taken that beauty, twisting and distorting it into something dark and frightening.

The evidence was all around them. Cherry trees lined either side of the path, but instead of delicate pink blossoms the petals that fell from them were pitch black, leaving a carpet on the ground like a void into the abyss. None of them said or acknowledged it, but they were all careful to walk around these areas.

At his side, Meera was walking with her head down, occasionally throwing the odd sideways glance at Hina, and Takashi wondered if something had happened between them. He wished more than ever that he was able to intuit her feelings and was just about to broach the subject at last when she spoke in an undertone, so that none but he could hear.

'It has… It has been so hard without you…' she whispered. Takashi looked at her desolately; he wanted to pour out his fears and doubts right then and there, but it was clear she had more to say.

'Ever since the Council took me back, I have felt more… separate, more… alone than I have ever felt,' she continued. 'And it is only getting worse. I had hoped it would have been different with you, but… I can no longer sense the feelings of other wolves. The longer I bear this gift unwillingly, the more I feel it pulling me away from you, away from our world, away from… from life…'

Takashi stared into her eyes with a mixture of pity and love and solidarity.

'I need you to know that you are not alone,' he began fervently, 'will never be alone as long as I draw breath. We are connected, we always have been, and whatever is happening to you is happening to us both. Since the Council took you back, my senses have been off too and I… I have lost the surety that once drove my decisions. I am ashamed to say that when Kaito first found me, I was hesitant to return with him. I did not know that what he said about you was true, and even if it was, whether coming back was the best thing for you. But I am here now.'

He stopped still in the centre of the path and they turned to face each other.

'I do not know if our pairing is meant to be,' he said. 'It felt that way once, but now I cannot say for sure. It seems we are always pulled in different directions, so who can tell what hand – if any – is guiding us. But what I can say is this; I will always fight for you – will always fight for us – until my last breath, and if at the end of all that we remain apart, then I will have died knowing I fought for the being most precious to me in this world.'

Meera stared into his eyes and for the briefest of moments, Takashi could feel the love radiating from her, then her head drooped as shame overcame her once more.

'I want nothing more than to be with you too,' she said brokenheartedly. 'But I fear I am putting you above the lives and wellbeing of so many. You have no idea what it was like to live with the Council like this – being looked upon as this broken, selfish thing. I wish sometimes I could simply embrace this gift for the good of others, even if it meant losing you, but some part of me beyond my control will not let it happen. I have never felt more weak or powerless in all my life…'

'It is not weakness,' Takashi said forcefully. 'There is nothing weak about wanting to live your own life, free from the rule of others. It is weakness to accept a life that is not of your choosing and do nothing to change it. Forging your own way is always the most difficult path – but it is the only path worth walking – and we two broken things will walk it together.'

Meera looked up at him and for the first time in a long time, he saw a glimmer of hope in her eyes.

'All we can do is hope the Senzo can transfer the gift,' she said, 'to fix us both and the problems we have caused.'

Takashi was about to say more when a voice hailed them.

'Hurry up – we can't stand around all day!'

Takashi and Meera turned to see Jaroe, Hina and Kaito watching them from some distance further up the path.

'Sorry – we're coming!' Takashi called and, after a quick glance at each other – filled with hope and determination – they hurried after the others.

Once they had regrouped, Jaroe cast an annoyed look at them.

'We do not have time for idle chatter,' he said angrily. 'You more than any should know that. If you wish to talk then you could at least…'

'Hey!' Hina cut across him. 'I saw something…'

They froze, staring ahead.

'Where is it?' Jaroe whispered. Hina nodded north-east at an area just off the path.

'Somewhere there, shapes moving amongst the trees…'

Jaroe stared at the place she had indicated.

'Well, then perhaps we should…' But Hina cut him off again.

'I sense fear… a terrible fear…'

For a moment she stood transfixed, every nerve of her body jangling, then, without another word, she took off after them.

'What are you doing?' Jaroe hissed after her. 'Come back here!'

But Hina was already darting off the path and into the trees. With an exasperated snarl, Jaroe set off after her and the others swiftly followed.

As they rushed along in Hina's footsteps, they began to notice steam clouding the air, cutting off visibility and bringing with it an uncomfortable humidity that was in some ways a relief after the freezing cold they had endured earlier.

'Must be a hot spring nearby...' Kaito murmured.

The steam grew so thick that soon they could barely see each other, but after pressing on a little further, they were swiftly through the worst of it and found themselves standing alongside Hina and faced with a stunning sight. Kaito's presumption had been correct. A large and beautiful hot spring stood before them, its edges lined with mossy boulders and its deep blue pool fed by a short, narrow waterfall that made a delightful tinkling sound. Sculptures and miniature shrines were dotted here and there and a small island with a flat rock for relaxing upon stood at its centre.

Steam rose invitingly from the water's surface as they stared at it in wonderment.

'If this is what spirits get to experience on their final journey then count me in,' Kaito said with a laugh. Jaroe, however, was not in the mood for jokes. He marched up to Hina and stared at her severely.

'I expect this kind of behaviour from the younger ones, but not from you,' he said furiously. 'What did you think you were doing...?'

But Hina did not seem to have heard him as she stared across the hot spring into the clouds of steam beyond.

'They're over there…' she muttered quietly.

'What are?' Jaroe replied irritably.

As one, the rest of the group followed Hina's gaze and stared across the water. As they watched, the thick, swirling steam parted and for a moment a dreadful scene was revealed to them. In a small clearing just beyond the hot spring, a foal spirit stood with its back against a rock. It was hunkered down, trying to make itself as small as possible as fear consumed it.

But it was not alone…

Four deer spirits had encircled it and were advancing out of the steam, tightening the net around their prey. These were no ordinary spirits – the sickness had taken them, turning their proud and noble forms into something diabolical.

Where there should have been dainty hooves there were now lethal talons. Where their bodies should have been dappled brown they were black as charcoal. Where their snouts should have been there were instead gaping, pitiless maws and where once beautiful antlers crowned their heads there were now gnarled, twisted branches, sharp as knives.

Their hollow, black eyes were fixed on the foal as they closed in around it, readying for the attack, delighting in its fear. The foal darted to one side – trying to break through them – but was swiftly repelled and backed-up against the rock once more.

'We must help it!' Hina said desperately, her eyes never leaving the foal.

Jaroe turned on her.

'This is not our fight...' he said sternly. 'We will help neither the Council nor this place by getting injured. You will *do nothing.*'

Hina continued to stare at the foal as the deer approached striking distance.

'I cannot sit idly by...' she said, bringing an angry snarl to Jaroe's lips. 'I must do what I can.'

With that she bounded away, scrambling over the boulders at the edge of the spring as she forged a path towards the foal.

'Does *no one* care about our mission but me?' Jaroe growled furiously as he set off after her with Takashi, Meera and Kaito close behind.

The four deer had reached the foal and now dipped their heads, presenting the terrified creature with a wall of deadly antlers that pressed in around it. Their tips were just grazing the foal's flanks when Hina appeared like a bolt of lightning, knocking one of the deer aside and tearing through its throat before the others had even realised what happened.

The remaining deer turned to face them and were advancing on Hina – steam swirling around them – when the others arrived and launched themselves into the fight.

What followed was swift and brutal.

Without heed to her own safety, Meera darted forward and bit into the hind leg of one of the deer, narrowly avoiding its lethal kicks and distracting it enough for Takashi to leap at it from its blind side and rip through its chest.

To one side, Jaroe and Kaito were facing another deer, pouncing when they could to bite and tear, and falling back when it swung at them with its antlers. In a daring move, Kaito goaded the deer into a charge and it lunged towards him, only for him to scurry aside at the last second, leaving it to crash headfirst into a tree. That was all the time Jaroe needed to spring onto its back and bite into its neck.

Hina found herself facing the final deer. This one was wily. It stood with its back to the foal, which had been frozen in fear since the fight began. The deer pawed the ground aggressively, warding off every attempt she made to get in close with its vicious antlers. Finally, she made a desperate lunge – but it was ready. It spun and lashed out at Hina with the talons on its rear legs, narrowly missing her as she veered away just in time, stumbling in the process.

As Hina slid onto her side, the deer turned to face the foal and mercilessly swung its antlers toward it, spearing it in the hindquarters. Its squeal of pain dragged Hina back to her feet and she leapt at the deer, but this time it threw caution to the wind and ran, with Hina hot on its heels.

Kaito made to pursue her but stopped and looked back at Jaroe.

'Should we go after her?'

Jaroe watched her go breathlessly.

'No,' he replied. 'We cannot risk losing the path or getting separated. She will find her way back to us.'

The pitiful cries of the foal were now all they could hear as the sounds of Hina's pursuit dwindled away. Anxiously, Takashi and Meera hurried over to the foal and looked down at it.

It was in a bad way.

The foal, a female, tried to stand as she looked up at them fearfully, but collapsed back to the ground. Slowly, so as not to scare her further, Takashi bent his head to inspect the wound. A tine from the deer's antlers had snapped off and was now embedded in the foal's hindquarters. As gently as he could, Takashi gripped the tine in his teeth and pulled it out, the foal squirming in pain beneath him.

The moment it was free they knew they did not have long, for around the edges of the wound a black, oozing substance like sentient tar could be seen worming its way inside.

This, then, was how the sickness was spread spirit to spirit – via wounds.

'No...' Meera breathed. 'We have to help her!'

Takashi stood frozen as he stared at the wound. Normally his response would have been innate, instinctual, led by the feeling that had always guided him – but without it he did not know how to act. He steadied himself. *Seven breaths...* He would need to make a choice...

In... Out... I must do something... I cannot let her turn like the fox... *In... Out...* But is it too late...? Is she already infected...? *In... Out...* I could suck out the sickness... But what if it infects me instead...? *In... Out...* If I turned, I could hurt my friends... But if I do nothing, what does that make me...? *In... Out...*

Five breaths – he had made his decision.

Without pausing to discuss it, he bent his head to the wound and began to suck out the sickness while Meera stared at him in shock. Once he was sure he had it all, he spat onto the ground and watched as the sickness wriggled its last and dissolved into the dirt.

For a moment he stood there while the others looked on aghast. He was breathing hard – tense and terrified – as he waited for the sickness to take hold, but as the moments ticked by in the horrified silence, he felt no change, and gradually began to relax. After a few minutes there was a collective sigh of relief from the group and Meera stepped towards him.

'Are you alright...?' she asked.

'I... I feel fine,' he said shakily. 'I think I got away with it...'

'That was a very brave thing you did,' Meera said quietly.

Together, they watched as the foal got awkwardly to her feet and stumbled off into the forest, away from the path of the Pilgrimage.

'Where do you think she's going?' Meera asked. Jaroe moved to stand beside her.

'Still so young...' he said. 'She is probably looking for her mother – she is not yet ready to take the Pilgrimage...'

A sound behind made all four spin around, but it was only Hina returning.

'I got it,' she said with feeling. 'How is the foal?'

'She was injured, but Takashi sucked the sickness out,' Kaito began, causing Hina to glance at Takashi with newfound respect. 'The foal got up and...'

'Never mind the foal!' Jaroe cut across him angrily, turning on Hina. 'You disobeyed me! You could have put our whole objective at risk! You do realise that if we fail then the Council fails with us? I will not have wolves on my Council who cannot follow simple...'

'It was the right thing to do...'

Jaroe stopped speaking and turned.

'What...?'

Kaito stepped forwards.

'It was the right thing to do...' he repeated. 'Our duty is to guard the domain, protect the innocent. If we shirk that duty once, when does it end? Hina made the right choice... the only choice...'

Jaroe stared at him in bewilderment. Just what was his game? If he was correct about Kaito – and his behaviour was just an attempt to impress him and gain favour in order to ascend the Council hierarchy – why go against him in this way? How would that serve his purpose? How would that in any way ingratiate him or gain his trust? Yet again, this young wolf had left Jaroe feeling confused and uncertain, and he did not like it...

Jaroe ignored Kaito and faced Hina.

'In future you will obey me, understood?'

Hina met his gaze unflinchingly.

'I will do what I have to,' she replied simply. Jaroe held her gaze a moment longer, then turned and headed back towards the path.

'We have wasted enough time,' he called over his shoulder. 'Let us return to our objective with no further distractions.'

As he walked away, Hina cast an appreciative glance at Kaito, then set off after Jaroe. Kaito watched her a moment, then proceeded to follow, with Takashi and Meera close behind.

Once they had regained the path, they continued north with Jaroe and Hina some distance ahead. Takashi and Meera caught up with Kaito and walked alongside him.

'What do you know about her?' Meera asked Kaito quietly as she stared fixedly at Hina. The whole incident with the foal had thrown Meera's perception of her. Perhaps there was more to her than the morose, aggressive front she put up.

'More than I perhaps should,' Kaito replied after a few moment's pause. 'It has never been a problem for me, but normally we wolves do not speak of our past lives, so when she told me her story, I... I was taken by surprise. I cannot explain it, but it was like... it was like a dam burst within her and it all just flooded out – I am not even sure she knew who she was talking to. At points I almost stopped her, but it seemed... cathartic for her. I have not told a soul what she said, but I feel you deserve to know... to understand...'

This is what Kaito told them:

A long time ago, in the land south of Agrath's Deterrent – the great wall that split the country from east to west – Hina had been a female warrior for a provincial lord, a rare occurrence in this world of men. She was one of the strongest and bravest fighters to have ever lived and was feared and respected for her integrity, her intellect and her prowess in battle.

When her master fell gravely ill, he released her from his service mere days before his passing, and she was left to wander the wilderness for many years. Initially lost and directionless, she eventually realised that she had been set free – free from a life of service to one man in favour of a life of service to all. It was a life free from the yoke of others – a life that she could choose. For the first time, she could go where she wanted, do what she wanted, live how she wanted.

From that moment on, she spent her days aiding the weak and unfortunate wherever she found them – fighting corruption and injustice in all its many forms and building a reputation greater and more far-reaching than the one that preceded it – a reputation for compassion and selflessness, instead of one of wile and lethality.

Then, one day, while wandering the outskirts of a small village, Hina came across a group of local thugs torturing a young wolf. Unable to stop herself as usual, she intervened, but her emotions got the better of her and she failed to mind her surroundings. She managed to kill the thugs, but not before one of them – unseen during her approach – had snuck up behind and mortally wounded her.

As she lay dying, she noticed another wolf appear behind the one she had saved. As she stared at it through bleary eyes, she saw that this wolf, strangely, looked not just like a wolf but like a man also.

This was the Soul Channel.

A voice echoed in her mind as she stared at him. He thanked her for her courageous act – then he gave her a choice... She could move on from this world – leave it all behind for a well-deserved rest in the next place – or she could choose to stay and continue fighting for the protection of this land and its people.

Hina did not hesitate to reply.

Meera had been transfixed by the story and looked over at Hina with newfound respect and understanding. Kaito watched her too.

'She is one of the only non-Kurai warriors to ever be granted the right to return as a wolf,' he said quietly. 'She may not seem it at times – but she is one of the strongest and most compassionate souls I have ever known.'

Meera was about to respond when she realised that Jaroe had frozen ahead and was listening intently, Hina by his side. Then they heard it too – frantic footsteps approaching at speed.

'What is it this time...?' Kaito whispered.

As the sounds drew nearer, they crouched low – ready to pounce – and when they were almost on top of them, Hina made the first move, lunging towards the figure that burst onto the path and bearing it to the ground.

Both Takashi and Meera reeled in disbelief at what they saw, and Takashi had to find his voice quickly to prevent Hina from attacking.

'Stop! I… I know him!'

Hina backed away slightly and let the figure sit up.

'It's… It's Kamari…' Takashi breathed in amazement. But what truly amazed him was what happened next. Kamari stared back at him with a mixture of fear, surprise and bewilderment.

'Takashi…?' he panted. 'Is… is that you…?'

CHAPTER TEN

'You... you can understand me...?' Takashi gaped incredulously.

'I can hear your voice... inside my head,' Kamari replied breathlessly. 'You sound like... like you... I'd recognise your voice anywhere...'

Takashi stared at his best friend in astonishment.

'How is... how is this possible...?' he whispered. Jaroe stepped forward, his eyes fixed interestedly on Kamari.

'In Sen'i there are no barriers to communication,' he said. 'It is how we wolves could speak to Reo, a spirit – and a human at that. Apparently, it also applies to living humans as well.' Takashi and Kamari looked at each other excitedly, but Jaroe quickly added: 'However, I must tell you that it will not last once you leave this place...'

Takashi moved closer and sat next to his friend who was looking at the wolves around him, clearly still on edge.

'It's so good to see you!' Takashi said happily. 'But what are you doing here?'

Kamari stared back at him searchingly, as though trying to see through the wolf to the man he had known.

'I don't even know where here is…' he replied after a moment. 'There is trouble in Aigano and I followed a creature here to put a stop to it.'

'Trouble?' Takashi replied anxiously. 'What kind of trouble? Tell me everything!'

Kamari dropped his gaze as the weight of his problems hit him afresh.

'It is bad…' he said darkly. 'There is some kind of a sickness spreading through the village… it has already claimed one life that I know of…'

'A sickness…?' Takashi echoed as a horrible realisation began to dawn. He glanced at the others and saw that they had come to the same conclusion.

'It started with the animals, then the rice crop failed, and the children began to get sick… and then it infected the adults…' Kamari said hollowly. 'At first, I could not understand how it had started or how it was spreading, but I knew this was no ordinary illness… Then I saw with my own eyes what is doing this to us…' For a moment Kamari trailed off and began to absently scratch his arm as the horrific images flooded his mind. Then he looked at Takashi earnestly.

'You may not believe me, but… they are spirits… but horribly disfigured!' he said with a haunted look. 'I witnessed these dark creatures going house to house in Aigano – spreading their sickness – and so I tracked one here, hoping to stop it at the source. But as soon as I arrived, it attacked me… When I tried to defend myself, my blade passed right through it and so I… I fled. I found a torii gate somewhere back there and followed it, hoping to lose my pursuer, and that is how I ran into you…'

Takashi stared at him in consternation – *so the sickness had reached Aigano…*

'Are my… my…' he began shakily, instantly hating himself for thinking of them first.

'When I left, your mother and sister were both well,' Kamari said.

'And your family…?' Takashi added swiftly. 'Ellia… your children…?'

'They are worried of course, but are all well,' he replied.

'I am glad to hear it,' Takashi said with relief, 'and glad too that we ran into you, for this is no place for a human.' Here he glanced around, indicating the forest in which they stood. 'You are in Sen'i – the spirit realm – and right now you are standing on the path of the Pilgrimage, the last journey a spirit ever takes. I will explain our reason for being here later, but we discovered this sickness shortly after arriving. Whatever this is, it is ancient – unseen for centuries – and any spirit it infects becomes twisted and violent. We do not yet know the source and we know only that it is spread spirit to spirit via injury, but it has clearly started to spill out into our world.'

'I have seen these spirits possess both animal and human and leave sickness in their wake,' Kamari said distantly, his battles with the ox and Akai replaying in his mind. 'So that is how it passes from spirits to the living, but given how fast it spread, I fear that once in the living, it may also be transmitted via touch or proximity or… Gods know what…'

'We are seeking a being who may know more about this sickness and its spread,' Takashi continued. 'He is known as the Senzo and it is our hope he can tell us how to fight it, and also help us with our own problem…'

'Then we have not a moment to lose,' Kamari said, getting to his feet at last. 'We must find this Senzo at once. Aigano is teetering on the brink – one gust and it will fall – and I cannot let that happen.'

Jaroe, who had been listening intently to Kamari's words and was now staring at him approvingly, nodded towards the route they had been travelling.

'It is this way, come,' he said, as he resumed following the path.

Kamari straightened the swords at his side and was just making to follow Jaroe when Takashi interjected.

'Wait! Kamari, it is not safe for you here… You will not be able to defend yourself – it would be safer if you were to…'

'I cannot go back,' Kamari cut across him. 'I *will not* go back without an end to the sickness. I must see this through to the finish…'

With that he set off after Jaroe, with Hina and Kaito a little way ahead. As Takashi looked on worriedly, Meera appeared at his side.

'You could not have changed his mind – you know how stubborn he is,' she said wryly. 'He is a village leader now – he just wants to help his people.'

'If he gets killed out here, it will not help them...' Takashi said quietly.

'We will not let that happen,' Meera replied. 'Don't worry – he will be alright.'

After a reassuring look at each other, they hurried after Kamari and swiftly caught up to him as they walked the path of the Pilgrimage northwards. For a time, they were quiet, each wrapped-up in their own thoughts, then Kamari broke the silence.

'I am so glad you are together at last,' he said, glancing at Meera and then focussing on Takashi. 'I hoped and prayed that death was merely the next step of your journey and to see you both now, I... I am so happy for you.' Despite his worries, he smiled at them.

'I could never be certain, but I felt sure I saw you a couple of times after the funeral,' he added. 'But to be honest, I... I wondered if I would ever truly see you again...'

Takashi looked back at him sadly.

'I am sorry it has been so long,' he began. 'We checked in on you from time to time, to make sure you were well, but... things have not been easy for Meera and I since being reunited. A problem has arisen that concerns our whole Council and in truth, that is... that is why we came to Sen'i – not because of the sickness...'

'Is this the problem you mentioned earlier?' Kamari enquired. 'What is it?'

'Me...' Meera replied quietly, unable to look at them.

'What… what do you mean…?' Kamari asked anxiously. Meera was silent a moment before responding.

'As hard as I try, I just cannot accept the gift of being the Soul Channel and it is… it is killing me…' she said at last, in barely more than a whisper. 'We seek the Senzo to transfer the gift to another, or it could spell ruin for the Council…'

With Kamari listening attentively, Meera explained everything that had happened to them since the battle with Kichibei and their flight from the Council. At times she found it difficult to go on and Takashi would chip in to bridge the gap, but soon she had brought Kamari up to speed on their situation and had introduced the other wolves to him.

When she was done, Kamari looked at them sorrowfully.

'I am so sorry to hear what you've been through,' he said, casting an angry look at Jaroe. 'After fighting so hard and sacrificing so much to be together, it is an unjust outcome. The Council have their priorities, but they have no right to force their will upon you – this gift was not your choice and you have every right to refuse it. Let us hope the Senzo can indeed transfer the gift and if there is any way I can help you, I will do all I can.'

Meera bowed her head humbly to him.

'It is most appreciated,' she said.

They continued on in silence for a while when they heard Kaito's voice calling from the head of the group.

'Hey! So, it looks like the path has disappeared…'

They all hurried to catch up to him and quickly discovered what he was taking about. The path had indeed disappeared, dead ending by a wooden jetty that jutted out over a tranquil river flowing in the direction the path had been heading. Two small rafts were moored either side of the jetty, bobbing lazily up and down on the surface.

'Is this all part of the Pilgrimage...?' Kaito asked uncertainly.

Hina stepped onto the jetty and looked down at the rafts.

'It must be,' she said. 'There is nowhere else to go...'

Kaito turned to Jaroe.

'What do you think?' he enquired.

Takashi glanced at Jaroe, who was staring fixedly at the water, and for a split second he felt sure he saw something in his eyes – was that fear? But it was gone in an instant as Jaroe looked up and scanned the area, searching for alternatives and seeing none. Finally, he stepped forward and took command.

'It appears we have no choice,' Jaroe said. 'We will follow this river and see where it leads.'

With that, he hopped down onto one of the rafts and Hina and Kaito followed, leaving Takashi, Meera and Kamari to jump onto the other. They pushed off from the jetty and soon found themselves floating serenely down the river, watching willow trees pass by to left and right. Side by side, Takashi and Meera observed the spirits of dragonflies flitting over the water's surface and the ghostly outlines of fish meandering in the depths below. After the chaos of recent events, it was a welcome break to sit still and take stock – but it was not welcome for everyone…

In the other raft, Jaroe sat hunched at its centre – tense and rigid – flicking his gaze from side to side and flinching every time it bucked on the current. He had always hated water, but what he hated more was that – for the first time ever – there were others present to witness his fear. Up until now he had always been able to hide it – for wolves had little cause to travel on water – but the situation had forced his hand and now others would see his weakness…

Pull yourself together… his mind hissed at him. *Do not let them see you like this…*

Kaito, oblivious to Jaroe's discomfort, stood at the prow of the raft, drinking in the scenery and enjoying the gentle headwind that brought with it the smells of the forest.

'I'm sure this would be lovely,' he said, to no one in particular. 'You know… if it wasn't for the sickness and the spirits attacking us and all that…'

Kaito turned to face Jaroe who swiftly sat up and tried to appear at ease, but he was fooling no one.

'Are you alright…?' Kaito asked in concern.

'I'm fine,' Jaroe replied tersely. 'Leave me be.'

At this, Hina and Kaito shared a look, then returned to facing downriver.

Back in the other raft, Kamari sat cross-legged at the prow, staring thoughtfully ahead. He glanced to his right as Takashi sat down next to him and for a time, they shared a companionable silence, quietly enjoying the view together. After several minutes Kamari spoke without looking at him.

'I had never truly believed in spirits until this sickness,' he said, watching as a spirit fish leapt from the water and disappeared below the surface. 'I knew you believed, but all the myths and legends our elders would tell us, I just… I could never bring myself to see any truth in them. I have always believed in what I can see with my own eyes, what I can touch with my own hands…' He stared at his palms reflectively. 'When I learned of the wolves and the Council, it forced me to question many things – if a warrior can return after death then what else is possible? But still, the notion of spirits seemed beyond me. Knowing what I know now, I see it as a failing of mine… but it is one I am willing to work at…'

Takashi looked at him earnestly.

'It is not a failing to be grounded,' Takashi replied. 'You are a leader – you always have been. You focus on the tangible, on the here and now, on those things of vital importance to your people. If we all spent our time focussing on other realms and possibilities, then our world would swiftly fall apart. What marks you out as different to most leaders is your awareness of self and your willingness to seek change where many would shun it. That is the mark of a great leader.'

'I have always found it easier to believe in people than possibilities,' Kamari said after a pause. 'After the battle with Zian when you went in search of Meera, I believed in you and your faith in your path, but I am ashamed to say that I was not sure you would ever find her. I was not sure, as you were, that the legends surrounding the wolves were true and I... I feared I would never see you again. Then, later, at your funeral, when your... when your...' he struggled for a moment to continue. 'I saw something in the flames... I saw you – as you are now – and it was only then, even after everything I had seen with the wolves and the Council, that I truly believed a warrior could return. I knew then that my long-held belief in you was well-founded. But, like the last time, I could feel your path pulling you away from me and I did not know if I would ever see you again...' Throughout all this Kamari had been staring fixedly ahead, but now he turned to face Takashi seriously.

'Promise me,' he said. 'Promise me that when all this is over, even if we are unable to speak, even if we cannot communicate at all, that we will see each other again... That this journey together will not be our last...'

Takashi stared back at his life-long best friend and saw through the tough, disciplined leader to the boy he had grown up with; the boy he had climbed trees and wriggled into fox dens with.

'I promise,' he replied firmly.

At that moment, a sudden impact buffeted the raft and Takashi would have been thrown into the water if it were not for the quick reactions of Kamari, who gripped him by the shoulders as he lurched forwards.

'What did we hit...?' Meera asked anxiously.

In the other raft, Kaito was staring fearfully into the water.

'There's something down there...' he hissed.

Hina, Takashi, Meera and Kamari moved to the edges of their rafts and peered into the water just in time to see a huge, dark shape pass within inches of them before disappearing back into the murky depths.

'We need to get off this river,' Hina said darkly. 'Now.'

'Is it just me...' Kaito began slowly, 'or are we going faster...?'

Hardly had he finished speaking when they all felt it. The current had gripped them in powerful hands and the ride began to get choppy. As one, they turned to face downriver and saw what they were approaching – but it was too late to do anything about it...

'Rapids!' Hina yelled. 'Hold on!'

With nothing to cling onto, they hunkered down near the centre of the rafts as they were pulled inexorably onwards, and entered the white-water...

In the blink of an eye their world became a maelstrom as the rafts were tossed upon the waves like leaves. Razor sharp rocks whipped by terrifyingly close and freezing cold water sloshed over the sides, drenching them. The raft bearing Hina, Jaroe and Kaito clipped a rock and spun – almost hurling them off – but they somehow managed to keep their feet.

Spray obscured their vision, but through the mist they saw something far worse than the fast flowing current and lethal rocks – for here and there, on the surface of the water, inky stains as black and viscous as tar could be seen floating. The sickness had even taken the river...

A huge swell passed beneath them, and for a second they were airborne, then they splashed back down and were showered with water as both crafts collided and ricocheted away. Hina turned to Jaroe and yelled over the din.

'What do we do!?'

But Jaroe was frozen in fear, his eyes rolling back in his head, his thoughts a whirlwind as chaotic as the river around them, and when Hina's voice reached him, it did so as if from a far distant place and he could do nothing to respond.

Hina glanced frantically from Jaroe to Kaito and saw in the young wolf's eyes a look of determination that took her by surprise. He was clearly thinking quickly as he looked around him, then – as though he had arrived at some conclusion – he moved to the back of the raft and dipped his head into the water.

'What are you...' she began to say, but then he raised his muzzle to reveal a bow line rope in his jaws. Biting through the end that had been attached to the raft, he swiftly did the same to the second bow line, leaving him with two long coils of rope.

Holding one of the coils, he moved as close as he could get to Takashi's raft and with a muffled: 'Catch!'

hurled one end of the rope across the gap to Kamari, who caught it in a firm grip. He then hurried over to Jaroe and with an authoritative: 'Hold this!' – that snapped him out of his paralysed state – passed the other end of the rope to him so that now both rafts were attached.

Gripping the other coil in his teeth, he passed one end to Hina and then – before anyone could stop him – leapt over the side into the pounding, frothing waves.

'What are you doing!?' Hina yelled around the rope in her jaws, but Kaito was already swimming as hard as he could for the bank, tugging the rafts slowly in his wake.

In breathless astonishment, the others watched his progress and Jaroe, still sitting hunched at the centre of his raft, could barely believe what he was seeing.

With incredible strength and resolve, Kaito inched his way slowly towards his goal but, unbeknownst to him, his time to reach it was running out…

A distant roar, heard by all except the fiercely focussed Kaito, warned of impending danger and, looking ahead, the others saw a terrifying sight. Through a fog of spray in the distance a jetty could be seen – clearly marking the end of this section of the Pilgrimage. But, blocking their way to it, was a vast whirlpool in the middle of the river, its sides slick with the tar-like sickness and a gaping void at its centre that dropped into utter darkness. Leaves, branches and fish alike could be seen being pulled relentlessly towards it, only to disappear from sight forever.

Oblivious to all this, Kaito swam on – muscles screaming, lungs burning, eyes stung by spray but somehow still managing to forge his way closer to the edge. Finally, he felt his feet touch the silty mud of the riverbed and hauled himself dripping from the water and on to the bank, glancing frantically from side to side as the rafts swiftly pulled away from him.

A pair of boulders caught his eye and he sprinted over, jamming the rope securely between them before turning back to check on the others. In the closest raft, the rope held by Hina pulled taut against the rock and she dug her claws into the wood to hold them steady. A moment later, the rope held between Jaroe and Kamari snapped taut as well, and only just in time…

As Jaroe and Kamari strained to hold them steady, the raft bearing Takashi, Meera and Kamari swung out over the edge of the whirlpool and teetered on the brink, the ropes barely holding them in place.

Seeing for the first time the peril they were in, Kaito gripped the rope between Hina and the boulders and began to pull with all his might, dragging the rafts painfully slowly towards the bank. In the furthest raft, Kamari was slowly but surely hauling their raft closer to that of Jaroe and Hina while Jaroe struggled to maintain his footing and his grip on the rope, his eyes squeezed shut with exertion.

Standing beside the sweating and straining Kamari, Takashi and Meera looked on – helpless and afraid – when Meera chanced to look upriver and saw something that froze her blood. Beneath the white-crested waves and the pools of sickness that floated like oil, a familiar huge, dark shape could be seen surging powerfully towards their raft.

Meera had only enough time to yell: 'Look out!' before it collided with the raft, knocking Kamari to his knees and almost making him lose hold of the rope.

'What was that?!' he yelled, but the others had no chance to explain, for the answer presented itself less than a second later.

As they watched horror-struck, a nightmarish creature surfaced a few paces from their raft and stared up at them with wide, lidless eyes, black as pitch. Takashi's first thought was that it was a kappa – an amphibious demon thought only to exist in myth – but as it reared out of the water, he realised that it was in fact the spirit of a giant salamander, but hideously deformed by the sickness. Where normally a salamander would have mottled brown skin, it was instead jet-black and its usually sleek and streamlined form was bloated and swollen and covered in revolting pustules, the water darkening around it where they burst. As it advanced slowly towards them, its mouth gaped open – wide as its head – and its empty eyes watched them desperately, hungrily.

When it was within two paces, it made its move – lunging at Takashi and Meera, who only just leapt aside in time before retaliating with tooth and claw, barely keeping their feet as the raft bucked under the salamander's weight. Glancing over his shoulder, Kamari glimpsed the beast for the first time and began to haul on the rope harder than ever, closing the gap between the two rafts inch by painful inch.

Back on the bank, Kaito watched in terror as the attack unfolded and somehow found the strength to redouble his efforts, hauling with all his might to pull them to shore while Hina and Jaroe clung on desperately – blood dripping from their mouths, the wood splintering beneath their claws.

With an almost superhuman effort, Kamari managed to pull them within jumping distance of the other raft and turned quickly to Takashi and Meera, who were biting and slashing at the salamander but doing little to stem its fury.

'Jump across!' he yelled at them. 'Now!'

A vicious series of attacks from the two wolves drove the salamander back, and in the momentary lull they moved to Kamari's side where Meera leapt across the gap to land safely on the other raft.

'You next!' Kamari yelled.

'What about you?' Takashi shouted back.

'I'll be fine, go!' his friend replied.

With a nod, Takashi surged forward and bounded across the gap where he immediately turned to look back. Now the last one on the raft, Kamari glanced behind to see that the salamander had leapt fully out of the water and was plunging towards him. With not a moment to lose, he steadied himself and jumped towards the other raft – and only just in time – as the salamander crashed down onto his, smashing it to splinters.

Kamari hit the water a little short of the raft and would have been dragged away if it were not for his firm hold on the rope. With Takashi and Meera helping Jaroe, they soon had him in reach of the raft and he was able to pull himself aboard. But they were not out of the woods yet – they were still some distance from the bank…

As the salamander struggled in the wreckage of the raft, Takashi and Meera hurried to help Hina, gripping the rope in their jaws to relieve some of the strain while Kaito valiantly continued to pull them closer and closer. When they were within a few paces of the bank, Takashi glanced at Hina.

'Go!' he mumbled around the rope. 'Go now!'

Exhausted, Hina nodded and – using the last of her strength – leapt to the bank and collapsed to the ground.

'Now you!' Meera yelled at Kamari, who clumsily got to his feet and jumped the gap too. Takashi turned to Jaroe.

'Jaroe, you next,' he said, and Jaroe, looking exhausted and shell-shocked, merely nodded and bounded to the bank. Takashi and Meera were left looking at each other.

'I'll be right behind you,' he said. 'Go!'

She held his gaze a moment longer, then jumped and made the bank. As she turned back, she saw that the salamander – still wreathed in wreckage – was bearing down on Takashi.

'Takashi!' she yelled. 'Jump!'

As Takashi crouched low and sprang forward, the salamander crashed through the raft a hair's breadth behind him and in an instant was further tangled in a mass of debris. As it struggled to stay afloat, the salamander was dragged towards the whirlpool and then – without a sound – vanished into the vortex.

Wet and bedraggled, Takashi stumbled up the bank and fell in a heap on the ground beside Hina and Jaroe. Kaito approached them wearily, his jaws red with blood where the rope had cut him.

'Is everyone… is everyone alright…?' he panted, slumping down beside them.

'You… you saved us all…' Hina said breathlessly. 'That was… incredible…'

'You were so… so brave…' Meera chimed in raggedly.

'Thank you… Kaito…' Takashi breathed exhaustedly.

'Yes… thank you…' Kamari added. 'What you did was… almost beyond belief…'

From his prone position, Jaroe watched Kaito in barely disguised astonishment. The ingenuity and level-headedness the young wolf had displayed – when he himself had been too terrified to act – had been… exemplary… Had he been wrong about him all this time…?

But when the others looked at him to say something, he found – not praise springing from his lips – but instead: 'We can't lie around all day – we need to keep moving.'

Getting shakily to his feet, Jaroe headed off in the direction of the jetty they had seen beyond the whirlpool and, after sharing a look of weary surprise, the others tiredly followed him. They soon reached the jetty where the path of the Pilgrimage continued in a northerly direction and, with aching limbs, began to follow it once more.

With Takashi and Kamari walking beside Kaito to further congratulate him, Meera found herself alongside Hina, who was watching Kaito with unbridled respect.

'That was a brave and selfless act,' she said quietly. 'He risked his life for us – put aside all thoughts of self to help others.' Hina turned to Meera, her eyes now blazing with anger. 'How does it feel to stand beside one such as he?' she hissed. 'To see an act like that in the flesh while you selfishly reject the gift of the Soul Channel? My entire life was spent doing all I could to help others, but you… you would *dare* risk the welfare and continuance of the Council… and for what...? Hmm? For what? What gives you the right to say "no"...?'

This was not the first time Hina had said such things, but this time, when Meera turned to her, Hina was surprised to see a fire burning in her eyes – a fire of anger and desperation and longing. Meera was about to respond when a cry up ahead from Kaito stopped her.

'You've got to see this!'

As they hurried forward, an amazing sight was revealed to them. Just off the path, a huge and beautiful waterfall fell into a calm pool, the water as green as moss. But it was not the waterfall that held their gaze, it was the figure standing at its base, shrouded in spray…

CHAPTER ELEVEN

'Is that…?' Hina whispered in awe.

'Yes…' Jaroe replied reverently. 'That is the Senzo… We've found him at last…'

For the moment, the Senzo seemed unaware of them as he stared out across the pool, so they took the opportunity to survey him from afar. From his garb and bearing, the first impression he gave was that of a priest, but unlike every other creature they had met in Sen'i, he did not have wispy outline of a spirit… no, he was something else entirely…

He was dressed in a white silk tunic over wide, hakama trousers of the same material, which were belted round his waist with a sash. On his head was a tall, black, peaked hat inlaid with gold and on his feet he wore loose wooden sandals. But it was his face that held their attention. Somehow, he looked both old and young at once. One moment he was a wizened old man – face lined with many lifetimes of care – and the next he was a spry young man with doll-like skin and eyes alight with boundless intelligence and compassion, but regardless of what he looked like, he always maintained an alert and upright posture.

As they continued to stare in wonder, an ageless voice echoed out across the pool.

'You can come closer – I don't bite, you know.'

After sharing a brief look of surprise – and not a little trepidation – the six comrades made their way over to the Senzo and bowed before him, not daring to look up.

'Come, come – there is no need for that,' he said, signalling them to rise. 'Too many people go through the world seeing only the ground at their feet – I will not have it in my presence.'

Hesitantly, they raised their heads to look at him and he gave them a weak smile – the older, wearier version of his face prominent as he did so.

'As you are no doubt aware, Sen'i finds itself in a grave situation that commands my attention,' he began distractedly. 'But obviously you would not have come here without reason – tell me how I can help.'

Without a moment's hesitation, Kaito stepped forward to speak.

'Senzo, we come to you with a grave problem of our own,' he began. 'Our Council is facing a...'

But he got no further as Meera nudged him into silence and shook her head. The Senzo watched them curiously but made no comment on this. After a moment's silence, Jaroe spoke, looking at the Senzo earnestly.

'Senzo, we wish to learn more about this sickness and offer any help we can to stop it.'

'Then you have my gratitude,' the Senzo replied, surveying them sagely, his face now prominently displaying the boyish, youthful side. 'But clearly there is more to your visit than you let on. Regardless, we must begin with introductions as you currently have me at a disadvantage.'

'My apologies for our rudeness,' Jaroe replied humbly. 'My name is Jaroe and I am the leader of the wolf Council. Next you have Hina, Takashi, our newest addition to the group Kamari – from Aigano village – and Kaito,' he continued, indicating each of them in turn. 'And lastly we have Meera.'

'Ah yes... Meera...' the Senzo said quietly.

He considered her a moment, a thoughtful, faraway look in his eyes, then turned back to Jaroe.

'Now we have introduced ourselves, I can tell you what I know, and it is not good news...' he began, his voice betraying no worry – not due to a lack of empathy, but a calm and resolute belief that the problem would be solved. 'When this sickness was first detected, we knew it was ancient and powerful, but now I have had chance to investigate, I have discovered it is far worse than we feared. What we are facing is... a Kaikru...'

'A Kaikru...?' Kaito echoed uncertainly, and even Jaroe looked puzzled by this.

'I would have been surprised if you had heard of them,' the Senzo said. 'A Kaikru has not been seen in these lands for centuries. They are vile creatures – demons that live only to spread suffering, disease and death.'

The Senzo looked away from them, out over the pool. They followed his gaze and, for the first time, saw with dismay that the surface of the water was stained here and there with the sickness, and it was spreading…

'Worst of all is the fact that a Kaikru does not come into being naturally,' the Senzo continued. 'Someone deliberately made themselves this way… It is an ancient and powerful ritual that must be performed above the clouds where the Gods cannot see, beneath the blood moon. For someone to have such hate in their heart to unleash this on the world, it…'

But the Senzo got no further, cut off by the sudden sounds of rustling and cracking branches approaching their location. With a snarl of rage, a monkey spirit – horribly twisted by the sickness – leapt from a nearby tree straight at the Senzo before any of them could react. But they need not have worried, for the Senzo caught the monkey as though it were nothing more than a toy and – placing a hand on its forehead as it struggled violently – closed his eyes and began to mutter under his breath. Slowly, the monkey's frantic convulsions began to ease and – like a dark cloud drifting aside to reveal the sun – the sickness dissipated, and its pure soul shone through once more.

The monkey hopped down to the floor, chattering happily, and the Senzo knelt down by its side. For a few moments he spoke to it in a low voice, then he rose to his feet and ushered it away and the monkey disappeared amongst the trees.

The wolves and Kamari had watched all this in quiet amazement, but now Jaroe stepped forward and spoke for them.

'You… you can cure it…?' he asked in wonderment. The Senzo turned to them with his aged side to the fore and they were surprised to see that he appeared older and wearier than ever.

'Yes…' he replied slowly. 'I can cure it… but it is spreading so fast, and with every spirit I heal my strength dwindles. I have been tracking the Kaikru and it is clear now that it is following the Pilgrimage, infecting everything it encounters. The Kaikru's cowl is the source of its sickness – it draws from this and its touch alone is enough to infect a spirit. This spirit can then infect others – even you wolves – by wounding them. Worse still, if one of these spirits were to possess a living creature, it would leave the sickness in its wake to spread through the living – plant, animal or human alike – akin to a plague…'

On hearing this, the wolves looked anxiously at Kamari who had not said a word this whole time. He raised his eyes and stared at the Senzo hollowly.

'It has already happened…' Kamari said, his voice barely audible. 'My village… Aigano… the sickness is spreading there… soon everyone and everything will be infected. I came here to find a cure, to put a stop to it – I cannot let my people die.'

The Senzo registered no shock or anxiety at these words but looked at Kamari with compassion. As he pondered this new information, he seemed to reach a conclusion.

'Yes… perhaps that is its ultimate goal…' he said thoughtfully. 'I fear I may have been blinkered in my investigation – perhaps its target is not Sen'i at all but… your world…'

Kamari stepped forward desperately.

'Then please… come back to my village – help me cure this!'

The Senzo shook his head sadly.

'My power is diminished,' he replied. 'I would not have the strength to keep up with the spread. No, the only chance you have is to cut off this sickness at its source – by killing the Kaikru. Without his influence it will cease to spread and cure all those infected.'

'Then tell us where to find it!' Kamari said forcefully. 'Tell us where and I'll kill it myself!'

The Senzo looked at him approvingly.

'You have a strong spirit,' he said. 'Your village is lucky to have you.'

He turned and faced away from them, looking along the path of the Pilgrimage.

'I believe I know where the Kaikru is going… and what its intention is… It is heading for the Overlook.'

'The Overlook?' Takashi asked in hushed tones. 'What is that?' The Senzo turned back to face them.

'The Overlook is the last stop on the Pilgrimage,' he began, a tremble creeping into his previously steady voice. 'The last stop before the Pilgrims leave here forever to be at peace. If the Kaikru can get there, it may be able to close off the Pilgrims' ability to leave Sen'i, giving it more spirits to infect, so it can spread its plague further and faster.'

At that moment the Senzo stumbled and almost fell, but Kaito rushed over to steady him.

'Thank you,' the Senzo mumbled as he eased himself into a sitting position. For a moment he was silent as he caught his breath, the others looking on worriedly. Then at last he spoke.

'Your arrival here is fortuitous,' he rasped. 'I do not think I would be able to finish the Pilgrimage to face the Kaikru. It seems obvious that I need not ask you to face it for me, so instead I will give you this advice. As I said, the Kaikru's cowl is the source of the sickness – remove this and its ability to spread it will swiftly vanish. Above all else, do not let its hands touch you – that is how it infects its victims and even you wolves are not immune. Follow the path of the Pilgrimage to its end and I am sure you will find it there.'

The Senzo lapsed into silence and Kaito turned to face the others.

'We do not know how many we will face – we should fetch the Council!'

At this, the Senzo raised a hand and shook his head.

'No… no you would be too late,' he said hoarsely. 'It is past the Spirit Hour – the doors to your world are shut and to wait for them to open would give the Kaikru all the time it needs. If you are to stand any chance, you must go now.'

Takashi, Meera, Kamari, Hina and Kaito all turned to look at Jaroe, awaiting his response. For a moment he appeared torn, staring at the ground in front of him. They had come here with a single objective – a mission to save their Council from collapse – but now a new and greater danger had emerged that threatened not just the wolves, but their whole world. It was a call they could not ignore. Whatever the cost to the Council, it was their duty to protect the domain from all threats. They would just have to hope – should they manage to survive this – that the Senzo would see fit to reward them and help solve their problem.

Finally, Jaroe glanced up at them all.

'We do as the Senzo says,' he intoned resolutely. 'It is up to us now to stop this Kaikru.' Here he turned respectfully to the Senzo. 'We thank you for your advice and hope to see you when the battle is done.'

'You will,' the Senzo replied, without a hint of fear or doubt. 'I am sure of it.'

With that, Jaroe nodded and headed off towards the path of the Pilgrimage. The others swiftly followed him, casting reverent and grateful looks at the Senzo, until only Takashi remained. He was just passing the Senzo when he stopped him with a word.

'Takashi,' the Senzo said, his voice weak. 'I see your struggle. I know what you have lost and how hard it has been. Always remember – do not fear making choices, mourn not making them…'

The Senzo turned away from him then and looked out over the pool upon whose surface the sickness still spread. For a moment Takashi stood frozen, wanting to reply, then, quietly, he continued on, his thoughts afire with unasked questions.

How did he know? he thought. *How did he know how difficult making decisions has become? How do I go on without the feeling? How do I find my way along my path...?*

With his mind in turmoil, he barely noticed as he stepped onto the trail of the Pilgrimage once more and followed after the others.

CHAPTER TWELVE

They had been walking in silence for several hours and for the first time became aware of a seasonal change around them. As though the Pilgrimage led its followers on a full yearly cycle, they found themselves in an autumnal scene, the foliage around them a rich array of reds, browns and yellows – save for those trees taken by the sickness that cast a pall over all around them.

At the head of the group, Kaito was walking alongside Jaroe, looking a little baffled as he ran through their encounter with the Senzo in his mind.

'I don't understand why we didn't tell the Senzo of our problem,' he finally said in bewilderment. 'Is that not why we came?'

Jaroe was about to reply when Meera, a few paces behind, got there before him.

'The Senzo was weakened – it was not the time…' she said quietly.

'It is clear now that this Kaikru is a much greater threat,' Jaroe added. 'It must be our sole focus.'

'I do not disagree with that,' Kaito said. 'But we could at least have told him – given him time to think on it while we fight to stop the sickness.'

'If we are successful then we will address if after,' Hina said firmly from behind Jaroe. 'The Senzo would not let our efforts go unrewarded.'

At the back of the group, Takashi and Kamari strode side by side, both wrapped-up in their own thoughts and unaware of the conversation going on ahead. As though awaking from a trance, Takashi realised he had barely spoken with his friend since being reunited and decided to seize the opportunity.

'I never had the chance to offer my congratulations,' he said, watching as Kamari emerged from the depths of his thoughts at these words. 'Your children are beautiful. Meera and I saw them on one of our visits – you and Ellia should be most proud.'

'We are indeed,' Kamari said with a small smile. 'You know, we… we named them after you and Meera.'

For a moment Takashi was speechless, then he bowed his head gratefully to Kamari.

'I am honoured,' he said, his voice humble.

'They can be a handful at times,' Kamari replied with a laugh, 'but Mia keeps them in check. She has become something of a role model for my children and the others in the village. At times I don't know what we would do without her. Your mother too – she is always there when we need her.'

Kamari looked away from Takashi, off into the trees.

'She misses you, you know – Mia,' Kamari said quietly, turning back to his friend. 'We all do.' At the distressed look on Takashi's face, he quickly added: 'I do not say that to make you feel bad, it is… it is just to say that… you have not been forgotten, and never will be…'

Takashi was silent for a moment as his words sank in.

'It brightens my heart to know that,' he said at last. 'And I wish I could say the same, but I feel my memories drifting away. That life feels so long ago now, I can barely remember it. It is like… it is like trying to hold onto a handful of dirt and stones… No matter what I do, I feel the dirt slipping between my fingers until only the stones – the big memories – remain. The memories of you and my family, of our triumphs and losses – but how much longer I can hold onto these, I… I do not know… but I will fight to keep hold of them until my last breath…'

Kamari was about to respond when a disturbance above made them look up.

A small flock of nightjars, still grouping together even in Sen'i, burst from the foliage with a loud chirruping and flew ahead of them, their luminescence pale against the thinning tree canopy. Captivated by the moment, all six of the companions fell quiet to watch as they flitted about, whirling and dancing in the weak light, seemingly leading them around a bend in the path.

As they rounded the corner, still spellbound by the sight, the nightjars split apart like a star exploding and vanished back into the trees. As the eyes of the group refocussed on the void left in their wake, they found themselves staring at an amazing spectacle. Not two hundred paces ahead of them a huge and imposing temple stood, towering into the sky.

Flanked on both sides by an impassable mountain range, the temple rose five storeys off the ground in the style of a pagoda, built mainly of crimson-painted cedar wood. The lowest level was reached by a steep flight of stone steps leading to a large veranda and the main entrance. The second storey was demarked by another railed platform from which worshippers could look out over Sen'i. Each subsequent storey above this was marked out by glorious, sweeping, black-tiled roofs from which ornate lanterns hung and the top-most roof was surmounted by golden metalwork of an intricate design.

It was beautiful indeed, but it was directly on their path…

'I see no way around it…' Hina said, glancing from left to right. 'We must pass through the temple.'

'Agreed,' nodded Jaroe, stepping forward. 'But be careful – we could easily be trapped in there…'

They approached the temple cautiously and soon found themselves ascending the stone steps in its cold shadow. Once at the top, they stopped and stared at the main doors which were built of the same, red-painted cedar as the building and were hinged and studded with highly polished gold.

'No sign of the sickness…' Takashi murmured.

'That does not mean it is not here,' Jaroe replied. 'We know the Kaikru must have come this way – keep your wits about you.'

Kamari strode forward and, with an effort, heaved open the doors, revealing a breath-taking sight within. As the group moved tentatively inside, they found themselves standing in the main prayer room and it was truly a wonder to behold. The space was cavernous, the colours a luxurious blend of reds and golds and blacks. Myriad gleaming pillars supporting ornately carved crossbeams ran the length of the room to left and right while the highly polished marble floor reflected back their awed expressions with near perfect clarity.

The main shrine was directly opposite them at the far end of the room, but in alcoves on both sides – partially hidden behind beautifully-painted paper screens – there were many smaller shrines, designated for personal and private reflection. Every shrine had several cushions laid before it and incense burned in holders at each, making the air thick and heavy, and more than a little soporific.

There were no windows save for on the front wall; instead, the room was lit by hundreds upon hundreds of candles that lined the walls and floor, creating pathways through which they would have to navigate. A chill draft from the open door set the candle flames wavering and shadows cavorted on the walls and pillars around them.

While the beauty of it all was captivating, what really caught their attention was the silence. There was not a sound to be heard anywhere, and not a single soul in sight…

As though drawn on by unseen hands, the group fanned out and slowly, quietly, began to make their way down the room, discovering new and wondrous details as they advanced. On one wall, Takashi discovered several murals depicting scenes from the Pilgrimage thus far. There was the torii and the hot springs, the river and the waterfall pool, and... Takashi stopped and stared hard at the last mural. It depicted what looked like a cliff edge overlooking a valley – a sight they had not yet seen.

Kaito appeared at his side.

'Do you think that could be...?' Takashi began.

'Yes, it must be the Overlook!' Kaito said, finishing his sentence for him. 'I guess we will find out for sure in time...'

In the centre of the room, Meera gazed around as she walked, taking in the many exquisite banners bearing the characters for peace, fortune and wisdom. Having been raised alongside the Kurai – who honoured no gods or spirits – she had never before set foot in a temple and for the first time ever, felt deep regret at this fact. The atmosphere was unlike any she had ever encountered. Even with everything that was happening, she felt calm, peaceful, reflective...

She had never before questioned her people's rejection of worship. Indeed, the concept of worship was so alien to her upbringing that the thought to question it had never even entered her mind. As she strode along in the tranquil silence, she realised that religion and worship was yet another aspect of her life she had never had control over; that she had never had a say in, one way or the other.

On the right side of the room, Hina was lagging behind Jaroe throwing sly glances at her companions. When she was sure no one was looking, she ducked into one of the alcoves and bowed before the shrine, her eyes closed. It had been such a long time since she had last had chance to pray. It ate away at her every moment she was without it.

In her past life, when she had served her lord, she had felt no need for worship. Like the Kurai, she had looked for nothing more in the way of the warrior than what was already there. But when she was released from his service and decided to live her life in service to all, she soon discovered religion and had embraced it wholeheartedly. It was the feeling of connection to everything around her that she cherished most about her newfound faith. It nourished, guided and comforted her, and now she could not imagine her life without it. Like most of the wolves, there were details of her past life she could no longer recall, but her faith was not one of these. She would never let it go…

'I promise to always do what is right…' she whispered. An image of Meera flashed across her subconscious and a snarl creased her lips. 'To always… *try* to do what is right…' she corrected herself. 'And to always help others before I help myself.'

She opened her eyes, blinking in the incense-heavy air, and glanced around to make sure no one had seen. Then she hurried after Jaroe, feeling like a weight had been lifted from her.

Slowly but surely, they all found themselves drawn to the main shrine at the far end of the room and were soon gathered around it, tracing the intricate details of its carvings and statues with their eyes. The incense was at its thickest here and hung in the air like a cloying fog that caught in the throat.

'I never fully understood religion and worship,' Kaito said, stifling a cough. 'But I guess, in many ways, it is no different to a warrior serving their lord – it is another form of all-consuming devotion.'

'It is more than devotion,' Hina said quietly, taking them all by surprise. 'It is faith; faith in something greater than yourself – faith that things will work out the way they should, and it inspires your faith in others...' Here, Hina shot Meera a nasty glance. Try as she might, she could never have faith in her.

'You sound like you have experience in this...?' Kaito asked interestedly. Instead of responding, Hina turned and walked away, heading out of the prayer room towards the back of the temple. After sharing a mystified look with Jaroe, Kaito and the others followed after her.

As they walked down the corridor leading off the prayer room, they passed many smaller rooms, partitioned by sliding doors and paper screens, but they did not have time to investigate them. They needed to exit the temple and continue on with the Pilgrimage.

A left turn at the end of the corridor led them to an expansive vestibule and there, on their right, stood the heavy wooden doors that would lead them back onto their path.

'Kamari, if you would be so kind,' Jaroe said politely.

With a nod, Kamari stepped forward and pushed against the doors... but to no effect. Bemused, he tried again, throwing his shoulder against it and heaving with all his might, but they were shut tight and would not move an inch. Kamari crouched before the keyhole and realised the problem.

'It's locked...' he muttered in frustration. 'Is there another way out?'

They glanced around but there were no other doors in sight, not even a window through which they could climb. Their only means of exiting the temple was blocked...

'There must be a key somewhere,' Jaroe said, looking back the way they had come. 'We must find it – we cannot dally here long.'

With Kamari in the lead – opening doors to each room as they passed – they slowly and fruitlessly searched their way back along the corridor until they arrived once more at the door of the prayer room.

'We will search here thoroughly before we move upstairs,' Jaroe said as he took the lead and entered the prayer room. 'Once we...' but he got no further as a strange sight caught his eye. Sensing his disquiet, the rest of the group hurried after him and soon saw it too. Through the drifting clouds of incense, something could be seen kneeling with its back to them at a private shrine on the opposite wall... It had not been there a minute ago...

As they looked closer, they could tell that it was human and dressed in the garb of a peasant. It was speaking in a low voice they could not discern, its head bowed devoutly. The group shared a nervous look while Kamari stared at it suspiciously. After a moment's indecision, Jaroe took a few cautious steps towards it.

'My apologies for troubling you,' he said, as formally as he could manage. 'We are looking for the key to the back door... might you know where it is?'

At his voice, the figure stopped speaking and a tense silence fell. For a moment it was still, incense curling around it, then it raised its head. The movement was slow, spasmodic, accompanied by the awful sound of bones cracking and scraping. Finally, it stopped, but it was not looking at them. Kamari's eyes were wide with shock – he knew what this was, but the words caught in his throat...

'You do not need the key...' it rasped, its voice a hideous death-rattle. 'For you will never leave this place...'

'Jaroe, move!' Kamari yelled, finding his voice at last, and in that same moment the figure whirled around and lunged. In the split second before it bore him to ground, Jaroe, and the rest of the group, were afforded a horrific snapshot of the creature's face. Like the spirit Kamari encountered on first entering

Sen'i, it had once been human, but was far from it now. As the rest of the group watched – paralysed with horror – they caught a glimpse of its whirling eyes, its hideously wide mouth, its neck bent at an unnatural angle, before it was upon Jaroe and they were hit with their own problem.

A loud, animal squealing rang out all around them – a chorus of voices filled with pain and suffering and fear – and the next moment, all was chaos as a pack of infected wild boar spirits burst through the wall at the far end in a shower of dust and debris. Bumping and jostling, they crashed heedlessly through paper screens and pillars alike sending candles flying in all directions as they charged wildly towards them.

'Kamari, stay out of the way!' Takashi yelled as the rest of the wolves turned to face this new foe.

'I want to help!' Kamari shouted back.

'There is nothing you can do!' Takashi replied. 'You cannot harm them!'

Nudging his friend towards a dark corner, Takashi leapt after the other wolves to join the fray, pouncing upon a boar as it passed and tearing into its neck.

Over by the private shrine, Jaroe struggled beneath the peasant spirit as it leered down at him – smiling so wide, he feared it would swallow him whole. Its strength was immense, but it seemed to take pleasure in his discomfort and was in no rush for the fight to end.

'I see loss in you,' it whispered, enjoying every second, its voice like the last gasp of a dying man. 'You struggle daily without him – you do not know how to lead without him...'

Jaroe thrashed more violently than ever, but could not break free.

'Your people see this,' it continued, licking its lips, its tongue long and black and forked. 'They see your weakness. You are nothing on your own... You are nothing without balance...'

Jaroe snapped at the spirit but it gripped his head and forced him down.

'Enough talk,' it said at last. 'Die...'

It bent its head towards him, its mouth opening wider and wider. Its tongue snaked out, flickering over his muzzle, but before it could bite down, something bulled into it. Jaroe caught a glimpse of brownish grey fur as it was knocked off him and tumbled to one side. Staggering to his feet, Jaroe turned to see Kaito standing over the peasant and – with one swift snap – snuff it out of existence.

There was no time for words, but in that moment Jaroe was prouder and more impressed by Kaito than he had ever been.

Restricting himself to a grateful nod, Jaroe and Kaito hurled themselves into the fight with the boar, whose numbers may have dwindled, but whose fury had not.

On the outskirts of battle, Kamari stared impotently at the life-and-death struggles going on before him. He had come here to help his people, so to be forced to stand idly on the side-lines was more than he could bear. He had to do something... He had to help in whatever way he could...

As he watched the melee, a faint glimmer caught his eye. Several fires had sprung up where candles had been knocked into paper screens and by their flickering light, he could see an object gleaming on the tusk of a boar, currently hovering on the edge of combat. As he looked closer still, he realised what it was – a key... Kamari's eyes lit up – he knew how he could help...

Slowly, stealthily, he prowled towards it, using any pillars still standing to cover his approach. He stopped behind one and peeked out. The boar was a mere handful of paces away with its back to him, shoving its comrades to try and gain access to their foe. The key swung from its tusk on a leather cord, tantalisingly close, and Kamari locked his eyes on it like a hawk.

Breaking cover, Kamari crouched low and scurried up behind the boar – his eyes never leaving the key. He stopped for a moment, heart pounding – so close now he could have plucked a hair from its back, and the boar was still not aware of him. Licking his dry lips, Kamari slowly – oh, so slowly – stretched out his hand towards the key.

At that moment, a vicious attack from Meera sent the nearby boar reeling backwards and the one with the key almost backed into Kamari, but he just dodged away in time. Regathering his composure, Kamari squared his shoulders and this time darted in, snatching the key from the boar's tusk and rolling away, before it even knew what happened.

'I have the key!' he yelled over the din, causing the others to look up. 'Let's go! Let's go!'

He was just turning to the exit of the prayer room when the boar leapt out in front of him, blocking his path.

On the other side of the room, Takashi looked over at his friend and took in his predicament in a heartbeat. Rapidly dispatching the boar he was facing, Takashi sprinted across the room – but was not quick enough…

With a squeal of rage, the boar charged at Kamari, moving faster than he would have believed possible. He tried to avoid it, but in the end, he knew it was futile. Takashi was only a few paces away when the boar sprang at his friend, plunging through his chest and exiting out the other side to land awkwardly on the cold marble beyond. Takashi was on it before it could regain its feet and bit through its throat, leaving it to shrink into the floor and vanish.

Terrified, Takashi hurried over to Kamari who stood frozen where he was, suddenly pale and wan. He staggered on the spot and almost fell but kept his feet.

'We must leave this place,' Takashi said urgently to his friend. 'Hurry – follow me!'

As though in a trance, Kamari stumbled after Takashi into the corridor beyond the prayer room while behind them the others brought up the rear, still locked in battle with the remaining boar.

Together, they reached the back door and Takashi turned to Kamari.

'Open it – quick!' he yelled.

Fumblingly, Kamari gripped the key and inserted it into the lock. For a second it looked like it would not turn, then the lock clicked and together he and Takashi shoved open the doors.

'Get out, now!' Takashi yelled. After a quick flurry of bites and swipes to gain some breathing room, the other wolves did as bidden and bounded through the doors.

As the boar regrouped and charged, all six of the comrades threw their weight against the doors and slammed them shut, feeling their foe crash into the heavy wood on the other side. As they struggled to keep them closed, Kamari slipped the key back into the lock and turned it. At that moment, as though they knew the chase was now futile, all sound from within the temple suddenly ceased and a ringing silence fell.

Exhausted, the group staggered down the stone steps at the back of the temple and Hina, Kaito, Jaroe and Meera collapsed onto the grass while Kamari took a few haltering paces away from them. Breathing raggedly, Takashi turned on him angrily.

'What were you thinking!' he yelled hoarsely. 'You could have been killed!'

Takashi was shaking all over – for a moment he felt sure he had lost his friend.

'Did you not think of your wife and children?' he added, angry and scared and relieved all at once. 'The village that needs you?'

Kamari was swaying on the spot and did not look at him as he replied.

'They are all I think of...' he said at last, his voice barely above a whisper. 'If you could see what this sickness has done to Aigano, you would understand...'

Takashi was about to continue his tirade, but at these words his anger faded away.

'You are right, of course,' he said in a low voice. 'I probably would have done the same thing...'

He let out a long, slow breath.

'Well... as long as you're...' But he never finished his sentence, for at that moment Kamari stumbled and collapsed to his knees. Takashi rushed over, swiftly followed by the others, and stared at his friend with concern.

'Brother, are you alright?' he said anxiously. 'Are you...' Takashi's eyes fell on Kamari's arm and fear gripped his heart.

'Roll up your sleeve...' Takashi said.

Slowly, knowing what he would see, Kamari lifted his sleeve, and there, sure enough, were the black nodules.

'Is that...?' Takashi breathed in horror.

'Yes...' Kamari replied hollowly. 'I'm infected...'

CHAPTER THIRTEEN

Kamari stared numbly at the nodules on his arm while Takashi strode back and forth in fearful agitation.

'No... no, no, no... this can't be happening...' Takashi said desperately. 'How do you feel?'

'I'm... I'm not sure...' Kamari replied hesitantly. 'A little... a little light-headed, but that's all right now...'

Takashi's eyes flicked here and there as he thought quickly.

'You said only one person had died from it so far...' he continued. 'How long before...?'

Kamari looked up but did not appear to see him, his eyes fixed and glassy as he responded.

'It was a young boy – Tayo...' he said faintly. 'He was the first to contract the sickness and passed only a few days later... but he had always been a frail, sickly child...'

Takashi continued his pacing as he digested this.

'So, we have time,' he said at last. 'Time enough to kill this Kaikru!'

Takashi stopped pacing and faced his friend.

'But you must go back to Aigano,' he added firmly. 'It was dangerous enough for you *without* this sickness sapping your strength. You must go back.'

Takashi turned to Kaito apologetically.

'Kaito… I am sorry to ask this, but would you…'

'No!'

Takashi looked at Kamari aghast. His blank expression had cleared and he was staring back at him with steely determination.

'I will not go back,' Kamari continued. 'I would rather die here and now than return with no resolution for my people! I am with you to the end…'

Takashi could see at once that there would be no dissuading him. He had seen his friend like this many times – all the way back to when they were boys – and it was pointless arguing. Takashi had never known Kamari to give up on anything in his life, and clearly, he wasn't about to start now. At least if Kamari was close by, he could keep an eye on him, and – if necessary – be there with him at the end... The mere thought made Takashi feel as though he were falling from a great height.

With a sigh, he looked at his friend and nodded.

'Alright,' he said quietly. 'But you stay by me at all times – I will not lose you.'

Kamari nodded back and got awkwardly to his feet.

'If that's all decided then we'd better move on,' Jaroe said. 'There is only one way we can go – follow me.'

With that, he turned and headed off along the Pilgrimage and for the first time, Takashi was able to take in the area around them. They were standing at the base of a narrow, steep-sided ravine that continued in a northerly direction from the exit of the temple. As he looked at the temple – which was no less stunning even after the events that occurred there – he could see that it was tightly sandwiched between the two sheer rock walls, funnelling any who wanted to walk the Pilgrimage through it.

It was a perfect ambush point... Takashi thought. *But what choice did we have?*

As he swung his gaze north along the mossy ravine walls, his eyes traced the path which was bordered at irregular intervals with intricately carved stone lanterns, their flames flickering dully. Looking further along the path, he could see what looked like bamboo trees growing in the distance beyond Jaroe's receding figure.

Good... he thought. He preferred the cover of trees. A ravine like this felt both too enclosed and much too exposed...

Nearby, Kaito wearily watched Jaroe as he marched stoically north.

'Does he ever get tired?' Kaito muttered as he got slowly to his feet and set off after him with Hina by his side.

Takashi turned to Kamari, unable to hide his look of concern.

'Are you able to walk?' he asked him.

'I'm fine,' Kamari said dismissively. 'Let's get moving.'

He set off and Takashi and Meera flanked him as he walked, ready to support him should he stumble along the way. Takashi could not help himself and threw worried glances at his friend every few paces, noticing his pale complexion and the beads of sweat on his brow. His gait was different too, his movements slow and stiff and his breath came in short, sharp bursts.

'Don't worry,' Takashi said reassuringly. 'You will be alright – I promise.'

Kamari swallowed nervously and looked down at him.

'I never told you,' Kamari began, 'but… I have a terrible fear of sickness…'

'I know,' his friend replied with a small smile.

'You know…?' Kamari gaped incredulously. 'But… how…? Did Ellia…?'

'You forget, my friend, I've known you since we were boys,' Takashi replied. 'There are no secrets between us. I could say your face is an open book, but in reality, it is more of a yelled proclamation,' he added with a chuckle.

'Are you saying I can't hide my emotions?' Kamari said sardonically.

'Well, who was it who almost got us executed by Lord Oran for speaking out-of-turn?' Takashi fired back with a laugh.

'Fair point,' Kamari mused as he recalled the incident. He then turned on Takashi with his best mock glare. 'So, what am I feeling right now?' he asked.

Takashi looked at him searchingly.

'That you want to beat me up for saying all this in front of Meera,' he said after a moment.

'You were right,' Kamari replied. 'My face *is* a yelled proclamation.'

With that, he made a playful lunge at Takashi and began to chase him along the path while Meera watched them with a smile.

It was not long before the ravine they were following abruptly ended on the outskirts of the bamboo grove Takashi had spotted earlier. The path snaked away between the masses of verdant green stems that stretched high into the sky, their lush foliage casting pale, dappled light on the forest floor. With the ravine behind and the bamboo stretching out before them, they could not have taken another route if they had wanted to. They would have to pass through the forest.

'There has been no sign of the sickness since the temple,' Kaito said quietly. 'Could the Kaikru have gone another way?'

'If it has, then there is a chance we could beat it to the Overlook,' Jaroe replied, staring into the serried ranks of bamboo stems. 'But I fear there is only one way there…'

Jaroe set off once more and Hina and Kaito followed, but Takashi looked at the forest warily. He had thought he would feel more comfortable under the cover of trees, but something about this bamboo grove made his skin crawl. He shook it off and proceeded after Kamari and Meera who had already entered the cool shade between the stems.

As they walked deeper and deeper into the forest, the ravine was soon lost to sight amidst the maze of bamboo that caused their vision to strobe everywhere they looked. Takashi's sense of unease grew and grew with every step he took and soon he knew why.

It began with a glimpse of movement out of the corner of his eye – an indistinct shape travelling low to the ground, darting between the perfectly upright stems that surrounded them. For a moment he thought he was seeing things, but then he saw it again and he froze.

'Did anyone else see that...?' he whispered.

'What?' Jaroe replied, suddenly on the alert.

'I saw something move…' Takashi hissed, staring at the last spot he had seen it. 'Over th…'

But before he had finished speaking there was a rustling behind them and they all spun to face it, just in time to see something slither along the ground and disappear out of sight.

'It's quick,' he breathed. 'It must have…'

But again, he was cut off as the rustling sounded, this time to their left, only to be followed by still more rustling to their right. They were surrounded.

What happened next happened so fast, they barely had time to blink, let alone move.

Without warning, the earth began to vibrate beneath their feet, causing leaves to rain down upon them. The vibration grew stronger and stronger, building in volume and intensity until they could barely stand and at the peak of its power, the ground suddenly exploded around them. From out of the shower of dirt and leaves and stones, they watched horror-stricken as thick, black, tendril-like creepers – possessed of the sickness – began to punch through the earth and wend their way purposefully between the trees surrounding them.

Moving with directed malice, the creepers began – with terrifying rapidity – to knit themselves together, forming ghastly, writhing, glistening walls from tree to tree and too late the group realised their intent. Before they could make any move to stop it, the creepers had come between them, forcing the six comrades apart and separating them into three groups: Kaito and Jaroe, Hina and Meera, Takashi and Kamari.

The rumbling vibration slowly diminished and at last they were able to hear themselves think and take in their full predicament. Each group was now standing in the corridor of a living, constantly shifting maze, whose walls were so high as to deter any thoughts of climbing out. They were trapped…

Standing in one such corridor, Jaroe and Kaito faced the direction they assumed the others stood.

'Is everyone alright?' Jaroe yelled.

'Takashi and I are fine!' Kamari shouted back.

'And Meera and I too!' Hina called.

'Good!' Jaroe replied. 'So long as we can communicate, we can…'

But at that moment, the walls facing Jaroe – facing each group – began to push in towards them, forcing them back, driving them further and further apart. Panicked, they pressed against the walls, trying to stop them, but at their touch the creepers grew vicious barbs, preventing any further contact. All they could do now was back away in dismay as the walls slid closer and closer, and finally came to a stop.

Stuck together, Meera and Hina looked around them fearfully.

'Can anyone hear us?!' Hina yelled into the sudden crushing silence. 'Hello?!'

She waited, but after several moments there was still no response. They were alone.

'What do we do...?' Meera whispered anxiously.

Hina looked back at her scathingly.

'We find a way out and regroup, of course,' she replied, and without further preamble she set off along the grisly corridor and took a left at the first crossroads. With a resigned sigh, Meera started after her.

They had been walking for several minutes when Meera became aware that Hina was muttering under her breath. She could not catch what she was saying, but from the tone it was obviously unpleasant. After enduring so many jabs and insults over the course of their journey, Meera's patience was wearing thin.

'Did you say something?' she asked, unable to hide an aggressive undertone.

'I was praying,' Hina barked back.

'I didn't know you were the religious type,' Meera replied mildly.

'I was praying,' Hina continued, ignoring her, 'for the strength to endure my time alone with you, praying for control over myself, praying for one iota of understanding of your utter, complete selfishness…'

Meera took all this with rising fury, but at the mention of understanding, she finally snapped. She stopped still at a crossroad in the maze and in that moment all her anger, all her pent-up sorrow and frustration, burst out of her like a torrent.

'Understanding!' she snarled in wrathful disbelief, taking Hina aback. 'You speak of understanding, but how could you possibly understand me? You know nothing about me! I have heard of your life before the Council once your lord released you, I have heard of the freedoms you enjoyed – moving where you would, living where you wanted, eating, sleeping and doing what you liked, never once being told what to do by anyone. Do you know what I would have given for even one day in your shoes? Do you have any idea what it is like to have your entire life mapped out for you, step by boring, tedious, mind-numbing step? I was the lord's daughter; every moment of every day of my life – from the clothes I wore to the food I ate – was already pre-planned and approved, written out for me like the script of some play. Choice was a foreign concept, love a vestigial word that had no bearing on who my father would pair me with. Rules and schedules dominated my life. Routine became the norm – surprise a forgotten concept – the days a blur of crippling boredom from which I could see no escape, no hope, no happiness… Takashi changed all that. In him I saw hope, in him I saw love, in him I saw the path through which I could forge my own life and make my own decisions, my own mistakes. He is the one thing I need in this world and this "gift" is keeping me from him. When you spoke of it earlier you asked: "What gives me the right to say, 'no'?" and I would say it is the fact that, once again – just as in my previous life – I was never given the chance to say, "yes"…'

By the end, Meera was breathing hard and Hina was looking at her with a mixture of shock and shame and sorrow. She had been staring fixedly into her eyes, but as her story finished, Hina hung her head and could no longer meet her gaze.

I am a monster… Hina thought remorsefully. *I have failed my faith. I should have shown her compassion, not contempt. There are always two sides to every story – it pays to read on…*

With her head held low, Hina spoke quietly.

'I'm so… so sorry,' she began, shame evident in every word. 'I have gravely misjudged you. It is no sin to want choice – it should be the right of all sentient beings. I have enjoyed it for so long now that I cannot imagine my life without it and I… I would fight to keep it. It is no wonder your body is rebelling against this gift – I am amazed you have held on this long. I thought you weak, but it would have been weakness to meekly accept it. You are far stronger than I ever imagined. I do not deserve it, but I humbly beg your pardon and will do all I can to make amends.'

Meera nodded in acknowledgement of her apology.

'I have wrestled with this for some time now,' she said. 'I know how this looks from the outside and I am not without guilt at how events have unfolded. But perhaps it is time to change how the Transference takes place – perhaps now choice should play a role…'

'I could not agree more,' Hina replied, finally finding the courage to meet her gaze again. 'And on the subject of choice… which way do you think we should go?'

Meera glanced down each of the crossroads and made her decision.

'Left,' she said firmly. Hina nodded and together they set off down the left path, forging deeper into the maze.

Some distance away, in another part of the maze, Jaroe and Kaito strode along in silence, wordlessly taking decisions at each branch in the path, but Jaroe barely saw the walls surrounding them. His mind was filled with the horrific visage of the peasant spirit, leering down at him.

'I see loss in you,' he heard it say again, the words echoing tauntingly.

How could it know...? he thought. *I tried so hard not to think about him – not to let it affect me...*

'You struggle daily without him,' it continued. 'You do not know how to lead without him...'

Jaroe shook his head, trying to dislodge the thought, but it would not leave him.

I don't need him... Jaroe tried to tell himself. *I can do this alone...*

'Your people see this,' the voice persisted malevolently. 'They see your weakness. You are nothing on your own... You are nothing without balance...'

Jaroe dimly became aware that Kaito was speaking but could barely make out the words.

I do not need balance...

'Jaroe...?'

I need no other...

'Jaroe... are you...?'

Jaroe snapped out of his reverie and turned to Kaito, who was looking at him worriedly.

'I'm... I'm sorry... what were you saying?' Jaroe asked.

'I was asking what we should do,' Kaito said, concern evident in his voice. 'How do we get out of here...?'

Jaroe looked away from him, his expression hollow.

'I don't know...' he said eventually. 'But *he* would have known...'

Kaito looked confused.

'Who...?'

Jaroe was silent a moment as memories he had tried to repress assailed him.

'Matai...' he finally whispered.

'Matai… He was before my time,' Kaito said slowly. 'But I have heard of him. I heard he was a great warrior.'

'He *was* a great warrior,' Jaroe said reflectively. 'He was my second-in-command on the Council, but he… he died during the battle with Kichibei. I did not want to admit it, but I'm realising now that I… I have not been the same since…'

'You were close?' Kaito asked.

'He was the best friend I ever had…' Jaroe said distantly, and then, with a smile, 'and the biggest thorn in my side. He would fight me on every decision – challenge me at every occasion – but I see now that I… I needed that… I needed someone… different to me… someone who would say what had to be said. Without it, I… I am struggling. I fear I have lost my way and the Council is suffering for it. I know my flaws and they are many, and I see now that I cannot do this on my own… I fear I cannot make the right decisions without him…'

Kaito stared back at him and there was a depth of understanding there that Jaroe had never seen before.

'He's in there, somewhere,' Kaito began, 'those dearest to us leave an imprint, deep down. Sometimes you can forget it's there, or even deny it. Sometimes you want nothing more than for it to leave you because the memories are too painful, but in the end, you never forget them, and it never truly goes away. I have only known you a short time, but you have already left an imprint on me. You know what to do, you always have done.'

In that moment, Jaroe saw clearly. Like a veil being pulled from his eyes, his senses cleared and for the first time in a long time he realised that he was able to intuit the emotions of another wolf. It had been so long that he felt drunk by it, revelling in the feeling, but one thing stood out with perfect clarity – he had been so very, very wrong…

All this time he had been suspect of Kaito's ambitions, assuming it to be a play at the Council's upper echelons, but on hearing his words, Jaroe felt he had been released from the depths of his isolation. At last, he could sense Kaito's genuine good intent and the lack of any ulterior motive, the suspicion of which had driven Jaroe to be aggressive to him from the start. Shame welled up in him as this thought struck, but he did not have long to dwell on it…

'Help!'

At this they both froze and listened intently.

'Can anyone hear me? Help!'

Jaroe and Kaito looked at each other in consternation.

'Meera!' Jaroe breathed. 'This way!'

With surety of purpose, Jaroe sprinted off – Kaito hot on his heels.

'Are you… are you alright…?'

Elsewhere in the maze, Takashi was looking at Kamari with concern. He had not spoken since the group was separated and was staring blankly ahead as they picked their way cautiously through the barbed corridors. At these words, Kamari blinked owlishly but did not look at him.

'I still feel it… inside me…' he replied after a time.

'What...?' Takashi asked perplexed.

'The boar spirit…'

As he said this, Kamari began to unconsciously scratch his right forearm, which Takashi could not fail to notice. It was a behaviour he had seen in Kamari since they were young.

'I could feel its pain and fear, its confusion and helplessness,' Kamari continued hollowly. 'Its world had shrunk around it to nothing more than a pinprick of anguish. But worst of all was its longing for it to end – one way or another…'

Kamari continued to scratch and already Takashi could see blood oozing down his arm.

'Is this what Tayo felt...?' Kamari said, in barely more than a whisper. 'Was this the last thing he experienced at the end...?'

Takashi stopped still, blocking Kamari's path, and looked up at him.

'I hope with all my heart it was not,' he began, 'but whatever the case, it will not be your fate – that I promise you. We will fix this… together…'

Kamari stopped scratching and met his eyes, but at that moment a yell cut across them.

'Help!'

Takashi spun towards the shout and found himself faced by a juncture in the maze with multiple paths leading off in different directions.

'Meera!' he called frantically.

Once again – where normally he would have acted instinctively – Takashi found himself paralysed by indecision as his mind bombarded him with questions and anxieties. Without the feeling to guide him, he was yet again faced with a choice to make – a choice Meera's life could depend on. If he chose wrong – or did not choose at all – Meera could be hurt or killed… His chest tightened – his heart pounding. *Seven breaths…*

In… Out… What can have happened…? Is she wounded…? How will I find her…? *In… Out…* You do not need the feeling… You are whole without it… Trust your instincts – you know where she is… *In… Out…*

Three breaths – he had made his decision.

'Follow me – this way!' he yelled at his friend as he sprinted off down the right-hand path with Kamari close behind him.

As he ran, Takashi felt his senses sharpen – whether through adrenaline or something else, he did not know – but he raced along taking decisions at each junction subconsciously as the calls for help grew louder and louder. As his anxiety grew, his speed increased until he was fairly flying down the corridors, ignoring the barbs that gashed his skin each time he drew too close to a wall.

At last, he turned a corner and found himself faced by a terrifying sight. He was standing in a large room in the maze, on the other side of which a life-or-death struggle was playing out. It was Hina, and she was in grave trouble.

It took Takashi a moment to process the events unfolding before him, but when he did, he knew they did not have long to act. Like a scene from a nightmare, he took in the creeper wrapped around the hind leg of the terrified, struggling Hina, the gaping hole in the earth it was dragging her towards and the frantic attempts of Meera to rescue her. Without hesitation, he leapt to join Meera – who was attacking the creeper holding Hina – just as Jaroe and Kaito appeared from another corridor and bounded to their aid as well.

Biting and gnawing, they desperately tried to chew their way through it as more creepers viciously lashed out to fend them off, and the walls began to close in around them...

Thinking quickly, Kamari cast about for a stick and soon found one, reaching into his pack for flint and tinder as the exits knit themselves closed and the room continued to shrink.

By now, Hina was mere paces from the yawning hole the creeper was reeling her towards as she scrabbled uselessly at the damp earth.

Tchk tchk – Kamari hurriedly tried to kindle a spark.

'Do something!' Hina yelled as her back legs neared the edge of the pit, but – try as they might – the creeper would not let her go.

A spark ignited, the stick caught light, a fire began to blaze.

Hina was now hanging over the pit as the barbed creepers sliced the air around her, holding the others back.

At that moment Kamari leapt forward, brandishing his flaming stick. He thrust it at the creeper holding Hina and, with a squeal of pain, it released her. She scrambled shakily out of the hole, but they were not out of the woods yet...

By this point, the room had shrunk to half its size and they had nowhere left to go. They had one chance remaining, and Kamari took it. Turning, he thrust his torch into one of the walls and it recoiled in pain. He swung it left to right and, with an animal shriek, the wall began to un-knit and soon there was an opening wide enough to admit them.

'Through here!' Kamari yelled. Needing no further encouragement, the group followed him as he ploughed a course through wall after wall. They were just beginning to wonder if the maze would ever end when they burst through another wall, and finally – against all hope – found themselves on the other side of the bamboo grove, back on the path of the Pilgrimage.

Breathless and bloody, they turned to look back and watched as the creepers gradually withdrew, shrinking into the ground and slithering away until no trace of the horrifying maze was left. They had made it through.

'Is everyone alright?' Jaroe panted. Hina's hind leg was bleeding and she was limping badly, but she shrugged it off and nodded.

'I'm fine,' she said, before – in a rare moment of vulnerability – adding, 'just a bit shaken – that's all.'

Kaito, who was standing a short distance from the group, spoke without looking at them.

'What do you think that is?'

The others turned to see what he was looking at and were surprised to discover a strange light ahead. It was a pure, blinding white glow that lit-up the sky directly on their path, calling them on. The horizon stood out starkly against its brilliance, but that is not what held their gaze – it was the strange figure standing at its centre. There was something about its posture... Something expectant...

It was waiting for them...

CHAPTER FOURTEEN

'There it is…' Jaroe murmured, his voice barely audible. 'The Overlook.'

'Then, that must be…' Hina began.

'The Kaikru…' Kamari finished for her; his furious gaze fixed on the silhouetted figure as he gripped his flaming torch tighter.

'It knows we are coming,' Jaroe said, still staring into the light. 'There is no point hiding. We must face it now. Are you all ready?'

He glanced around the group as each of them nodded in turn, their faces set and determined, the light of battle gleaming in their eyes.

Jaroe turned back to the glow.

'Then let us finish this,' he growled as he set off towards the figure in the distance.

Maintaining a tight formation, the group followed the path north, trailing long, midnight shadows, the light so dazzling that they could only snatch glimpses of the way ahead for fear of going blind. As they walked, Takashi became aware that Kamari was breathing heavily. The air rattled in his throat and he stumbled – almost dropping his torch

– as he stifled a cough with his hand. Although he said nothing, it was patently obvious – his condition was worsening. They had to stop the Kaikru now…

The group had been so fixated on their goal that it was some time before they became aware of the dark shapes on either side of the path. At first, they took them for rocks or trees but slowly, and with a prickling of horror, they realised these were no mere inanimate objects. They were spirits – sick spirits – staring transfixed at the light; rank upon rank of them – human beside animal, predator beside prey – all united in the twisted image of their creator.

'This is what it has been doing…' Jaroe breathed. 'It has gathered an army!'

The spirits seemed completely unaware of them as they passed, standing motionless as statues, their black eyes vacant and unblinking. Slower now, the group continued on and with each step they took, the light seemed to dim until they were able to discern more of their surroundings. A cliff edge revealed itself ahead and as they drew closer still, they were presented with a fabulous sight. An expanse of perfect white light stretched out before them, seemingly endless. At first it appeared blank and featureless, but as Takashi watched, he noticed details begin to appear – a building here, a rice paddy there, a river and a bridge – and before he knew it, he was looking out over Kohaku Valley – his birthplace – sculpted from light. He glanced at the others, noticing the same look of awe in their eyes, and wondered if they saw what he did, or something else entirely.

For a moment he was lost in its beauty, then – like a switch had been flicked – he spun back to face the Kaikru, still standing framed against the last of the dazzling light. Its back was to them – its nonchalance palpable – as the group came to a halt a short distance from it, poised and ready to spring.

Under their furious, wary gaze, the Kaikru straightened, its bones cracking loudly in the silence as it continued to stare over the edge. For a moment it was quiet, drinking in the view, then finally it spoke.

'Welcome,' it said, its voice the rumble of mountains shifting, the crash of waves on rock, 'to the Overlook. This was once the last stop on the Pilgrimage, a final chance for the Pilgrims to look out over their pathetic, worthless lives before stepping out into nothing and embracing whatever comes next – but not anymore…'

Slowly, with languid confidence – utterly at ease – the Kaikru turned to face them, stepping out of the blinding light and revealing itself at last. It was a sight that would haunt their dreams forever after. What stood before them had once been human but had been warped and twisted almost beyond recognition.

The horrific creature was tall and stooped and black as night, hunched under the weight of a long, trailing cowl that rippled and oozed like sentient tar – *the source of the sickness…* Beneath the cowl, four arms as thick as tree trunks hung loose – apparently at ease – but the massive fists were clenched tight in anticipation. Its feet, although humanoid, were gnarled and clawed, the sharp talons scratching furrows in the rock it stood upon. Like the sick areas of forest they had encountered earlier, the Kaikru's outline was oddly sharp and jagged – as though it had been cut out of mid-air – but an aura of roiling shadow surrounded it. However, it was the face beneath the cowl that drew their eyes with morbid, horrified fascination. Where there should have been a face there was instead a hideous, horned, crimson mask – infused with its flesh – split by a terrifying frozen grin set below two gaping holes through which the Kaikru's eyes blazed out like twin fires.

As it stared back at them with malevolent intent, two long, barbed tongues flickered out through its mouth hole, probing the still air.

'I can taste your fear,' the Kaikru hissed into the silence. 'Your desperation. Your longing to stop me. But you are too late... The Pilgrimage is closed. None may pass from this realm now save by my leave – and I have important work for them to do...'

After their initial shock, the group rallied at these words and Meera stepped forward boldly.

'Who are you?' she snarled.

The Kaikru seemed amused at the question, for a rasping chuckle escaped the mask.

'Who am I...?' it echoed slowly. 'For a time, I wanted nothing more than to forget – the shame I felt was worse than any physical pain an enemy could inflict. But then

I realised that to forget was akin to forgiveness – and I can never forgive. You asked who I am – I was once Gen Kichibei, but now… I am so much more…'

Takashi's eyes widened in shock.

He is Lord Shigako Kichibei's son…

In his mind's eye, Takashi was transported back to the battle outside Harakima and his final confrontation with Shigako Kichibei. As though from another's perspective, he saw himself – his human self – lying on the damp grass, bleeding from a terrible stomach wound as Kichibei stood over him with his weapon raised. He watched as Kichibei brought his blade scything down only for Takashi to punch his own sword through Kichibei's chest. But Kichibei did not fall and even as the breath died in his throat, he bent to deliver the killing blow. But the blow never came. Like a bolt of lightning, he watched as Meera bulled into Kichibei and knocked him to the ground, ignoring his feeble struggles as she bent to his neck and – with one swift bite – tore out his throat.

That was how Gen's father had died.

That was how his attempt to retake Hirono had ended.

That was why Gen was eaten-up with shame and had made himself into a Kaikru…

Takashi could see at once that Meera was thinking the same as he.

Did he know that the two souls responsible for his father's death were standing in front of him…? Did he even care…?

Overcoming her shock at this revelation, Meera took another step forward and glared at the twisted creature before her.

'Why are you doing all this?' she asked fiercely. 'What do you want?'

The Kaikru stared back at her, eyes blazing like furnaces, and raised his arms skyward. When he spoke, his voice was the roar of thunder crashing.

'Chaos!' he replied.

At this, the Kaikru's spirit army on both sides of the path suddenly turned in unison to face the six comrades, their black eyes fixed on them with feverish intent.

'If my family cannot have this land, then I will see it wither and die!' he boomed.

As one, the spirit army took a step nearer the path, narrowing the corridor through which the group had passed earlier.

The Kaikru was about to say more when Kamari broke out in a coughing fit that shattered the momentary silence. He covered his mouth with a hand and when he withdrew it there were spots of blood on his palm. The Kaikru stared at him curiously and pointed a massive fist towards him.

'You...' he began slowly. 'You are human... and here before your time... though I recognise my own work – you will be joining us shortly...'

The Kaikru's tongues slithered out again, tasting the air.

'You are from Aigano – are you not?' he continued. 'Have my scouts been having fun in your village? Is that why you are here?'

Kamari stared back at him with hatred in his eyes and held his torch higher, but before he could respond, Jaroe stepped forward, fangs bared.

'Enough talk – this ends now!'

With a furious snarl, he hurled himself at the Kaikru – but he was more than ready for this…

With lazy indifference, the Kaikru knelt to the floor, placing the fingertips of one hand to the cold stone. From these contact points dark tendrils sprang, scything through the dirt and rock in a hail of debris as they tore towards the charging Jaroe. The big wolf saw them coming but was too slow to respond as the tendrils burst forth from the earth, taking huge chunks of the rock with them and batting him away like a rag doll. Jaroe hit the ground some distance away and tumbled end-over-end before sliding to a stop in a bloody and bruised heap.

Seeing the fall of their leader, the rest of the group roared their fury and sprang at the Kaikru, but they were no match for him… Placing the fingers of his other hands to the floor he swiftly sent more tendrils their way, watching with amusement as they erupted from the ground to batter his enemies back. Kaito was the first to fall. After dodging a vicious swing from a chunk of rock, he attempted to break through the Kaikru's line, only to be knocked flying towards Jaroe who was getting shakily to his feet.

Hina was next. She had made it past the Kaikru's defences and was racing towards him – snarling fiercely – when a tendril punched through the earth beneath her, lifting her bodily and sending her arcing through the air to land beside Jaroe and Kaito.

A fierce body blow that cracked a rib sent Takashi skidding backwards, leaving only Meera and Kamari to face the Kaikru. Bobbing and weaving, Meera darted from side to side, keeping the Kaikru's attention on her and away from Kamari. A vicious swing from a tendril that missed her by a whisker opened a window of opportunity for Kamari – and he took it without hesitating.

Hefting his flaming torch with one hand, he drew back and hurled it as hard as he could at their enemy. With his focus intent on Meera, the Kaikru did not see it coming until it was too late. The torch hit him full in the chest and he recoiled in agony, the tendrils instantly disappearing back into the ground.

With a bellow of pain and rage, the Kaikru rounded on Kamari.

'You think you can defeat me!' he thundered. Bending to the ground once more, the Kaikru placed his hands to the rock and Kamari stumbled back in fear as a wall of slithering tendrils sprang up between them. The wall pushed forward, forcing Kamari and Meera back until they had regrouped with the others, but the wall kept on coming.

'I had not yet decided where my attack would begin,' the Kaikru hissed as it continued to repel them back between the serried ranks of sick spirits that watched them pass with silent ferocity.

'But now...' he continued. 'Now you have made that decision for me...'

By this point, the group had been forced to the outer edges of the spirit army by the ever-approaching wall, but at that moment it melted into the ground and they could once again see the Kaikru on the lip of the Overlook. Clear as day, his voice rang out, echoing off rock and stone – its intensity shaking their bones like an earthquake.

'We march for Aigano!' the Kaikru screamed. 'But first – kill them!'

As one, the Kaikru's army turned their way and surged towards them like a tidal wave – desperate, angry, agonised screams tearing from their throats.

'We cannot win this alone!' Jaroe yelled over the din. 'Run!'

Turning tail, Jaroe sprinted off south along the path while the others watched him go, breathing hard – unwilling to leave the fight. But, faced by this overwhelming horde, they knew he was right – without aid they did not stand a chance...

With the army of spirits bearing down on them, they raced after Jaroe and swiftly caught up with him, not daring to look back even a moment for fear of stumbling.

'What do we do?' Hina shouted, struggling to make herself heard. Jaroe turned to Kaito and Hina who were running to his left.

'You two – you must keep heading south! Find a doorway that will bring you out near the Council and gather them all – you must get them to Aigano as fast as you are able, for that is where the battle will be joined!'

Jaroe turned to face Takashi, Meera and Kamari, who ran to his right.

'The rest of us – we will cut east and look for a doorway that will bring us out near Aigano. We must alert the villagers and get them to safety if we can.'

Jaroe turned back to Kaito and Hina.

'Go now – you must not fail!' Here he looked directly at Kaito and whispered, so only he could hear. 'I believe in you.'

At this, Kaito radiated pride and determination as he nodded in acceptance. After a quick nod at Hina, the two wolves powered on ahead, following the path due south where they were soon lost in the haze.

'We go east!' Jaroe yelled to the others as he veered to his left. Within seconds he had left the path behind and was wending his way between the trees, with the rest of the group close on his heels and the spirit army sweeping along in their wake, casting a dark pall over the land.

As they ran on, dodging branches and leaping rocks and rivers, Meera asked the question they were all secretly thinking.

'What time is it?' she yelled over the pounding of their footsteps. 'Will the doorways be open?'

No one replied for they all feared the answer – but what choice did they have other than to continue running and hope for a miracle…

They lost track of time as they raced along, searching desperately for a doorway while the spirit army continued their relentless pursuit. With aching limbs and pounding hearts, their world became a blur of rocks and trees as fatigue began to overtake them. They had put some distance between them and their pursuers, but they knew it would not last.

It soon became apparent that Kamari was struggling. He was clutching his chest, the breath wheezing in his lungs, and finally he collapsed to the floor, his body racked by a coughing fit. Takashi skidded to a stop beside him and stared at him anxiously.

'Kamari! Are you alright…?'

Kamari wiped the palm of his hand on his kimono, smearing it with blood, and looked up at his friend.

'I'll be fine…' he replied, as he tried to get to his feet, swinging his arms for balance. 'I…'

But he stopped mid-sentence and turned towards where his hand had been. Slowly, he groped the air – there it was again! Cold…

'I feel cold air!' he said excitedly. 'I think there might be…'

He shifted position slightly to stare at the spot from a different angle.

'Yes!' he called. 'It's a doorway!'

Jaroe and Meera appeared beside them and Jaroe approached the spot.

'He's right! It is a doorway!' Jaroe said eagerly. 'There is no time to lose – let us pass through!'

Without waiting for a response, Jaroe leapt through the doorway and vanished. Takashi turned to Kamari and looked up at him.

'You know that once we pass through here, I… I will no longer be able to speak to you,' he said sorrowfully. 'Do not worry, we will deal with the Kaikru – I will not let his sickness take you. Just get the villagers to safety and please… be careful…'

Kamari looked at him determinedly.

'I will do what I have to for my loved ones,' he replied. 'As you always have.'

Takashi nodded in understanding.

'Whatever happens…' Takashi began, 'you will always be my brother.'

Kamari smiled back at him.

'Don't forget about us,' he said. 'We will never forget you.'

Bending down, Kamari placed his forehead against Takashi's, then stood and nodded at Meera before turning to the doorway unhappily.

'This was highly unpleasant last time,' he groaned.

'Just go through it, you big baby,' Takashi replied with a laugh. Chuckling, Kamari stepped through the doorway with Takashi and Meera close behind him and the spirit army still surging their way.

CHAPTER FIFTEEN

Meera, Takashi and Kamari tumbled through the doorway and got to their feet, shaking from the intense cold of their passage. Jaroe stood a short distance away, assessing their position, and they swiftly joined him. They were standing at the northern end of Kohaku Valley on the outskirts of Dengai Forest, at the top of the western valley slope. From their elevated position they could see Aigano lying still and quiet in the valley below, apparently deserted.

Looking out on their childhood home was a strange sensation for both Takashi and Kamari after all that had happened. For Kamari there was nothing but fear and guilt; fear that they may already be too late and guilt at having left them – guilt at having directed the Kaikru's attention towards Aigano. For Takashi it would be his first time setting foot in his birthplace since his new life began. He had seen it from afar when he checked in on Kamari and his family, but had not yet been within the boundaries and even from here, he felt the memories flooding back – memories he feared he had lost forever.

Jaroe turned to them and, with a decisive nod, darted off south-east down the steep valley slope towards the centre of Aigano, with Meera close behind him. Before following them, Takashi and Kamari shared a lingering look that was beyond words, a look of loyalty and trust and everlasting friendship. Then they sprang after the others with determination and clarity of purpose.

As they slid side-by-side down the muddy slope, the two friends were transported back to their childhood, to the carefree days before they had any concept of the evil that lurks in man's heart. Throughout their journeys together they had seen both the best and worst of man and, for better or worse, it had changed them deeply. But, in that moment, for the briefest of times, they forgot all that and were children again. Joy gripped their hearts with the sheer thrill of being alive as dirt and mud splattered them on their headlong ride. But, like all good things, it was over too soon as they reached the bottom of the valley, shook the mud from themselves, and pelted off after Jaroe and Meera.

As they hurried south-east, it became apparent that the village was eerily silent. It was still early, but Kamari had expected to at least see some signs of life. He stopped on the bridge and glanced around fearfully, the breath catching in his throat. Cupping his hands around his mouth, he yelled out loud, his voice echoing off the steep valley sides.

'Hello! Is anyone here?' He waited a moment but gained no response and so tried again.

'If you can hear me, please gather by the bridge immediately!'

Nothing happened and Kamari was beginning to fear the worst when he noticed faces appearing at windows and doors cracking open.

'Please! We do not have much time! Please gather at the bridge!'

Slowly but surely, the villagers began to emerge from their houses and approach the bridge, most of them coughing or wheezing and clearly unhappy about being in close proximity with others. As they drew near, they stared at Kamari and his three wolf allies with disbelief and suspicion.

When most of the villagers – or at least heads of households – had assembled, Kamari addressed them again.

'I am sorry for leaving the way I did, but I had to pursue a lead and did not know if I would return,' he began, his voice carrying strongly across the gathering. 'I went in search of the source of this sickness and together,' he indicated Jaroe, Meera and Takashi, 'we have found it. This may be hard to believe, but we are facing a Kaikru – a demon intent on unleashing chaos on our land and he is heading this way right now with an army at his back.'

At these words, anxious murmuring broke out amongst the villagers and Kamari had to raise his arms for silence.

'If we can defeat it, the sickness will be lifted, but to survive this you must all flee south at once!'

More murmuring spread through the crowd – the shaking of heads and hacking, spluttering coughing.

'We are too sick to travel!' one man called out. 'We will not make it!'

'And you will not make it if you stay!' Kamari shouted back. 'Gather your families, leave your belongings and flee – as your leader, I implore you!'

The villagers continued to glance at each other but made no move to leave, when an ominous sound echoed across the valley. Like the hiss of escaping gas, the sound grew louder and louder, the tone warping and distorting as pitch-black clouds began to amass to the north in the early morning sky, pulsing and roiling, gathering and growing like the smoke from a burning building. Thunder boomed overhead and the land beneath the clouds darkened, but as they peered terrified into the darkness, they were able to discern a deeper shadow moving across the ground like a tide – moving their way…

'They are here!' Kamari yelled as a crash of thunder rang out above them. 'You must go, now!'

Panicked screams spread through the crowd as they turned and rushed off to gather their families or immediately set off southwards down the eastern riverbank. With a quick glance at Takashi, Meera and Jaroe, Kamari sped off towards his home to find Ellia and the children.

Suddenly alone on the bridge, the wolves turned towards the approaching darkness side-by-side.

Faced with these impossible odds, they knew they had little chance of winning – but that did not mean they would go down without a fight...

As he watched the army thundering their way, Jaroe spoke without looking at his companions.

'I have been hard on you both,' he said quietly, 'and I do not want to die with bad blood between us. I pray that we make it through this so we can resolve our issues properly.'

He glanced at each of them in turn.

'Are you ready?'

Takashi and Meera nodded, their eyes never leaving their foe.

'Then let us do what we can to slow them.'

With a howl, Jaroe bounded forwards, exiting the bridge on the western bank and racing north towards the enemy with Takashi and Meera at his flanks. Thunder boomed again and lightning forked across the shrouded sky, illuminating the blanket of cloud that had been thrown over them.

'Remember,' Jaroe called as the peal of thunder died away. 'Do not let them cut you!'

To the charging enemy they made a laughable spectacle – three creatures against the might of an army; three small souls they had already witnessed their master effortlessly defeat. To their sickness-addled minds, these wolves were little more than pebbles in their path to be stepped on without noticing. But when they clashed, they paid dearly for their overconfidence.

When the two sides came together, it was like water breaking against a cliff. Takashi, Meera and Jaroe hurled themselves into the ranks of their enemy, knocking many smaller spirits flying and setting about them with tooth and claw to devastating effect.

Horrific, twisted figures leered at them from all sides – the shades of humans, horses, cattle and deer, jostling to get at them, driven by the pain and fury the sickness instilled. In the midst of the melee, a horse spirit faced off against Takashi. It reared onto its hind legs, its head and neck splitting vertically in two like an alligator's mouth to reveal row upon row of serrated teeth. It lunged at him, snapping at the empty air where he had stood not a moment ago. Rolling to one side, Takashi darted forward and knocked it to the ground where he tore into its chest and ripped out its heart.

Only a few paces away, Meera found herself face to face with a human spirit, dark as night – like a shadow without its person. He had clearly been a warrior once, but all shred of his honour and dignity was gone. Where his arms should have been there were instead long, needle-sharp knives with which he scythed the air before her, his eyes like empty wells in his vacant face. Ducking and dodging, Meera waited patiently for her opening and soon saw it, diving beneath a particularly wild swing before pouncing at his chest and tearing into his face.

On the other side of Takashi, Jaroe was locked in combat with a huge snake, bloated by the sickness, its tail tip split in three like a trident and lethally sharp. It had wrapped around his middle and was squeezing him tight while jabbing at him with its tail, which Jaroe was only just managing to avoid. Carefully baiting it, Jaroe waited for the next attack. As the snake's tail speared towards him, he ducked to one side, watching as it impaled itself, releasing him with an agonised hiss.

But for every spirit they dispatched two more would spring up in their place and there seemed to be no end of them. As much as they tried to prevent it, they were being forced back; back towards the bridge at the centre of the village, back towards the villagers who were still collecting their families and fleeing.

Before long they were once more standing on the bridge – the very spot where Takashi's journey had begun all that time ago when Zian's mercenaries were sweeping Hirono. Side-by-side, they faced the terrifying horde before them, blocking passage across the bridge.

'There are still people leaving the village!' Meera yelled over the din. 'What do we do?'

Jaroe glanced behind them and saw a young couple with three sick infants struggling to make their way south. There were no options left to them. It would be a fight to the death.

'We go out fighting!' Jaroe snarled. He pointed his nose to the sky, and he howled – a long, echoing note filled with honour and pride and determination. Takashi and Meera joined him and soon their howls rang out across the valley, their strength and ferocity briefly discouraging the spirit army amassed on the western bank.

Jaroe, Takashi and Meera stopped howling and waited for the sounds to die away – facing their enemies determinedly – but the howls did not fade… Instead, they grew stronger – rising and rising – a chorus of many voices ringing out in unison, promising for the first time in this battle something they believed they had no hope for – a chance…

'The Council!' Takashi yelled delightedly. 'They are here!'

And he was right. Approaching from the south along the western bank, the full force of the Council loped into view, sweeping across the grass with fierce and single-minded intent. At the sight of this unforeseen foe, the spirit army recoiled and had mere moments to gather their wits before the wolves were upon them, a wave of grey clashing with a wall of black in a whirling maelstrom of vicious combat.

Aching and weary, Jaroe, Meera and Takashi were about to re-join the fray when two familiar figures approached them – Kaito and Hina. Jaroe stepped forward and looked at them proudly.

'You did well,' he said, 'but how did you get here so fast?'

'We were gone so long, the Council came looking for us,' Kaito replied, glancing over his shoulder, clearly eager to join the battle. 'We met them on the southern border of Dengai Forest, so we did not have far to go.'

'You started without us,' Hina said wryly.

'Well, there is plenty more to go around,' Meera replied with a competitive glint in her eye.

Needing no second bidding, Meera, Hina, Jaroe and Kaito hurled themselves into battle, but Takashi stalled a moment. Some instinct told him to turn around and he did so, looking out across the village. As he watched, he saw Kamari emerge from the doorway of the healing house, leading Ellia and their two children and it gladdened his heart to see them alive. But then, two figures he had been desperate to see since he arrived in Aigano appeared from behind them – his mother and his sister Mia. Even from this distance, it was clear they had the sickness and his heart clenched in fear within him.

Just hold on a little longer... he thought. *I will not let you perish...*

As though she had heard his thoughts, his mother looked up and their eyes met across the expanse between them, an expanse that – in his reborn state – was more than mere distance. Somehow – against all the odds – the light of recognition danced in her eyes. She knew her son – would know his soul whatever form he took. She smiled at him – a smile of pride and love and encouragement – and Takashi felt his spirit soar within him.

He bowed his head to her, then turned, eyes alight with battle, feeling as if he could take on the entire army single-handed.

Thunder rolled and lightning split the sky, bringing with it ice-cold rain that pelted the ground, swiftly turning the grass to mud. With a howl, Takashi leapt from the bridge and ploughed into the enemy like a battering ram, joining his brothers and sisters from the Council to repel these monsters from his home.

He had just dispatched an ox spirit when a towering figure loomed over him and he stumbled back in shock. A humongous bear – ten feet tall – reared up on its hind legs and roared its pain and fury to the heavens. As he watched in horror, the bear's chest cracked open, splitting apart to reveal a gaping hole, lined with rings of jagged teeth that gnashed the air hungrily.

Takashi was just preparing to pounce when Kaito and Jaroe appeared at his side.

'Big fella, isn't he?' Kaito quipped.

'Big enough...' replied Takashi.

'We take it down together...' Jaroe said with a snarl.

The bear roared again and brought one of its shovel-sized paws swinging towards them, only to hammer into the mud where they had been standing a moment previously. Kaito darted around to harry its hind quarters and the bear spun with a sweeping backhand that caught him on the shoulder and sent him tumbling. Using the momentary distraction,

Jaroe leapt at the bear and bit deep into its right foreleg, and it bellowed in agony. With a mighty heave, it swung its leg and hurled Jaroe away, leaving Takashi to face it alone.

With his eyes constantly on its lethal paws, Takashi nimbly dodged its first swing but was too slow to avoid the second. It clipped him on the side of the head and knocked him to the ground and before he knew what was happening, he was being lifted bodily off the ground between the bear's massive paws, to be held in its vice-like grip. It began to apply pressure, gradually at first, but building and intensifying until Takashi felt his bones grating and his chest tightening.

Then, slowly, deliberately – savouring the moment – the bear drew him closer and closer towards the mouth in its chest that gaped horrifyingly wide, clamouring to swallow him whole. Takashi struggled with all his might, but could not break free. His hind legs were just grazing the lower teeth of its mouth when the bear snarled and glanced up. Takashi followed its gaze and saw Jaroe had clambered onto its back and was tearing ferociously into its neck.

The bear bucked violently – trying to dislodge him – but to no avail, and with its focus on Jaroe, it did not see Kaito approaching until it was too late. With lightning speed, Kaito zipped towards the bear and latched onto its throat. Attacked front and back, the bear finally released Takashi who crumpled to the ground, nursing his bruised and cracked ribs.

The bear stumbled around, swiping at the two wolves with ever diminishing ferocity until finally, with a last groan of pain, it toppled forwards, slamming into the wet ground and flinging Jaroe and Kaito to the earth.

Bruised and weary, Jaroe and Kaito looked at each other over their defeated opponent and Kaito could see the pride and admiration in the other's eyes. In that moment Jaroe finally realised what he had to do – but that would come later.

The next moment, Hina and Meera appeared beside them as Takashi got awkwardly to his feet, wincing in pain as his cracked ribs shifted. He turned to Meera anxiously and saw that her legs were shaking badly.

'Are you alright?' he asked her quietly, so that none of the others could hear.

'I could ask the same of you,' she replied. 'You were nearly crushed by a bear!'

'I'm fine, but are *you* alright?'

Meera sighed.

'Now is not the time for this, but… the gift is getting heavier,' she answered tiredly. 'I thought at first it had improved when you arrived, but now… it is weakening me every moment. I… I do not know how much longer I can hold out…'

'We are so close,' he said, taking a step toward her. 'We are so close to finishing this. If we can kill the Kaikru the Senzo will surely agree to transfer the gift. You just have to hold on a little longer.' Those words echoed in his head – the same words he had thought on seeing his mother and Mia. It felt like his whole world was hanging by a thread.

'I'll... I'll try...' Meera replied.

Hina stepped forward and addressed them all.

'We are holding our own, but there is no victory until the Kaikru is dead.'

She turned to face north and they followed her gaze, looking out across the remainder of the spirit army to where the attack had been launched from. Standing atop a rise in the distance – placidly watching the chaos unfold – was the Kaikru himself. He locked eyes with them and raised his arms, beckoning them on.

He wanted this.

He wanted them to attack him.

Then so be it…

CHAPTER SIXTEEN

'We need all of us,' Jaroe yelled over the din of the battle. 'It will take all we can muster to defeat this demon. We deal with his army first – then we take him down together!'

With a howl, Jaroe led the charge back into the fray and Takashi, Meera, Hina and Kaito followed after him, baying their war cries to the sky.

Many wolves fell that day, but far more of the sick spirits were blinked out of existence. They were not fighting through a will of their own but the will of the Kaikru, and Takashi could see the struggle on the face of each and every one he dispatched. He felt great pity for them and terrible remorse at what he was being forced to do, but it was the Kaikru who was the architect of their ignominious demise, not himself.

As more and more spirits were defeated, Takashi wondered what would happen to them as he dropped another to the mud and watched it melt into the ground. Without following the Pilgrimage to the next place, where would they go? Would they find peace beyond the tragic final moments of their existence, or would they face only nothingness...?

Few, if any, knew what lay ahead of those who stepped from the Overlook. But whatever it was, Takashi hoped these poor souls would have a chance at the same nirvana.

Worse than seeing the spirits fall was seeing wolves turn. Several had already been infected and put down by their comrades when Takashi faced his first. The wolf hit him like a spear, sending him tumbling sideways and was upon him in a flash. Takashi recognised him as one of the escorts that had led he and Kaito to the quarry, but the sickness had warped him. His black eyes gazed piercingly into his soul; his jaws slung with bloody slaver as he snapped viciously at Takashi.

'You can fight this!' Takashi yelled desperately. 'Don't give in to it!'

But the wolf was too far gone. His struggle with the sickness had already been lost. Short of imprisoning him until the Kaikru was defeated, there was no other way to stop him. As they wrestled viciously, Takashi summoned his strength and kicked the wolf from him, sending him sailing through the air to crash against a nearby rock and drop to the ground, limp and still.

'I'm sorry...' Takashi murmured.

He turned to look over at the village on the eastern bank, where he could still see several families making their way slowly south.

What is keeping them...? Takashi growled. *Hurry up!*

As selfish as it was, his one overriding hope was that Kamari had managed to get his mother and Mia – as well as Ellia and the children – to safety.

He looked away from the eastern bank to survey the battle and it was clear that the tide had finally turned in their favour. They had the spirit army on the back foot and were ready to press their advantage – but why had the Kaikru not stepped in to help? Why was he content to watch his army slowly dwindle?

Takashi was just turning to check on the Kaikru when an ominous rumble sounded that shook the earth beneath them. This unexpected occurrence caused a momentary lull in the battle as both sides struggled to keep their feet. The rumbling intensified; buildings shook, trees fell, the Daku River eddying like the sea.

'What is happening?' a wolf yelled on Takashi's left.

They did not wait long to find out. In the midst of the battlefield on the western bank a crack appeared, racing across the grass beneath the feet of the staggered wolves and spirits. Then, with an unearthly noise, the ground was torn asunder as a vast boulder punched through the mud like the tip of an iceberg, sending wolves and spirits flying in all directions.

Slowly but surely, the boulder continued to rise up as Takashi, Meera, Hina, Kaito and Jaroe regrouped to watch its terrifying progress. Moments later, the boulder hung free of the earth, dirt, pebbles, roots and rainwater cascading from it as it hung elevated above the crater it had left behind.

'How is it...?' Hina began to ask, but they all knew the answer.

As their eyes travelled down the boulder, they soon saw the dark tendrils supporting it, hefting it as though it weighed no more than a feather. Tracking them with their eyes, the group followed the tendrils north to where the Kaikru knelt, one hand to the ground, smiling wickedly.

'You creatures and your struggles are nothing to me!' he boomed, his voice seeming to emanate from the dark clouds above as lighting flashed, briefly illuminating his hellish form. 'My soldiers may fall but when you all lie dead, I will make more! This land will descend into darkness!'

With these words he raised the boulder higher off the ground and too late they saw what would happen. With a cackle of laughter, the Kaikru brought the boulder slamming into the earth, crushing several wolves and many more spirits who had no chance to avoid it. A second swing and more wolves fell, the boulder breaking apart into fragments that the Kaikru hefted and flung at his enemy with lethal accuracy.

'This is it,' Jaroe yelled across the battlefield in a voice no wolf could fail to hear. 'There is nowhere to run and nowhere to hide – for any of us! We have one chance, and one chance alone… We must rip the cowl from the Kaikru! Without it he will be powerless!'

A fragment of boulder hurtled past, but Jaroe barely flinched.

'Half of you stay here to face his army – the rest, with me!'

With another howl Jaroe raced off north – his eyes set on the Kaikru – with Takashi, Meera, Hina, Kaito and several more pounding along in his wake.

From his position the Kaikru could see them coming and chuckled to himself. He flexed his long, gnarled fingers – listening to the knuckles crack – and placed the fingertips of all four hands to the floor. His cowl rippled as he summoned his strength, then, with a roar, tendrils sprang from each of his hands, scything off in all directions to do his bidding.

At the head of the charging group, Jaroe saw the tendrils spreading to left and right – saw the danger they were running into – and knew they had no choice but to continue. Out of the corner of his eye he watched as the tendrils found their way to trees on both sides and dug deep into their roots, ripping them from the earth as though they were little more than twigs and holding them aloft and upright.

The Kaikru cackled – a grating, ear-splitting sound – then, as if the trees were hideous extensions of his fingers, he began to slam them into the earth on both sides of his advancing enemy, seeking to crush them into the mud.

As Takashi pelted along, he saw a huge cedar tree swinging towards him and just dived away in time, but another wolf running to his right was not so lucky. Leaves and branches showered him as he came within inches of being crushed, his fury mounting as the last dying yelp of the wolf pierced his heart.

More wolves fell as trees hammered the ground all around them, leaving huge furrows in the sodden earth they were obliged to leap over to continue their headlong charge. Meera was running just ahead of Takashi when a stray branch, dislodged from one of the trees, clipped her shoulder, knocking her to the ground.

Takashi hurried over to help her up, looking at her with concern, his chest heaving.

'Can you walk?' he asked, as she got painfully to her feet.

'I'm fine, I… Look out!' she yelled. Takashi turned to see a maple scything towards them and – as though of one mind – they rolled nimbly aside as it crashed into the ground, sending jagged splinters in all directions. They had no time to catch their breath and hurriedly got to their feet to resume their frenzied approach.

By this point most of the trees had been smashed to bits and the remaining wolves were closing on the Kaikru. But he was not out of tricks yet…

A huge, dark tendril whipped past the group, racing south towards the battle that still raged behind them. Glancing over their shoulders, the wolves watched in fearful awe as the tendril latched around the beautiful bridge at the heart of the village – the bridge Takashi had known his whole life, the bridge he and Kamari had fished from as children, the bridge upon which his father had died. With the creak and crack of splintering wood, the tendril wrenched the bridge from the riverbank and held it aloft. For a moment it hung there as the Kaikru revelled in the moment – delighting in the fear of his enemy – then he hurled the bridge towards them with all his might.

'Everyone, watch out!' Takashi bellowed as the shadow of its approach fell over them. Like a meteorite from the heavens, the bridge arced towards a clump of wolves who had been forced together to avoid the attacks of the trees.

As though in slow motion, Takashi saw the bridge impact the earth ahead; watched horror-stricken as the wolves vanished beneath an explosion of wood, stone and mud – lost to sight and lost to this world, further victims of the Kaikru's callous brutality.

The rain continued to pour down as Takashi and Meera skidded in the mud to avoid colliding with the debris and diverted around it, intent only on reaching the Kaikru. As they rounded the shattered remains of the bridge, they saw with anger and sorrow that of all the wolves they had started their approach with, only Jaroe, Kaito, Hina and one other – a young wolf known as Hideo – remained.

To the Kaikru they appeared a pitiful foe – he had beaten them once and he would do it again.

'That's quite close enough!' he roared, the tendrils snaking back to his fingers only to spring up again as a wall between them. Faced with this impenetrable obstacle, the wolves slid to a stop and soon found themselves being forced backwards, just like at the Overlook.

'I tried to live with it,' the Kaikru said in a low voice that nonetheless carried to each of them. 'I tried to tell myself my father died an honourable death. He died in battle, died fighting for what was rightfully his, but in the end, it does not matter what he fought for – he is still dead and my family dishonoured.'

With each word he continued to drive them back, back towards the melee between the remaining wolves and spirits.

'I should have been there with him,' the Kaikru continued. 'I should have fought alongside him – would have gladly died alongside him for a chance to look in the eyes of his killer.'

Takashi stared back at him through the mass of tendrils with furious contempt.

'Now's your chance,' he snarled as the Kaikru continued to drive them back. 'It was I.'

Meera appeared at his side, glaring ferociously at their enemy.

'It was us.'

'You...?' the Kaikru hissed in disbelief.

'Your father was a murderer and a coward,' Takashi spat back. 'A coward who tried to steal control of Hirono when Harakima was at its weakest – does that sound like the work of a great and noble warrior to you?'

'No...' the Kaikru breathed, still unconsciously forcing them back. 'It cannot be...'

'To protect our home, I would kill him a thousand times over!' Meera roared. 'You will soon follow him!'

By this point they had reached the outskirts of the battle, not far from where the bridge had once stood. The Kaikru stopped moving. He was breathing hard, still obscured behind his wall of tendrils. Then, with a thunderous scream of shame and fury, accompanied by a fork of lightning and a peal of thunder, he stepped out from behind his protective barrier to face them.

'I will make you suffer like nothing before!' he screeched, the clouds swirling above him like a vortex. 'You will beg for death before the end!'

With a guttural scream, he tore towards them, but he had not gone more than a few paces when a flaming arrow hit him full in the chest. Squealing in agony, he ripped it out and flung it away only for two more to follow, burying themselves in his stomach and shoulder. Both the wolves and the Kaikru looked around in surprise to see where they had come from and there, not far from the veranda of their house, stood Kamari and Ellia, longbows clutched in their hands and flaming arrows pulled taut on their bowstrings.

'Been a while since we last did anything like this together!' Ellia quipped to her husband. 'Shall we stick a few more in him?'

'Gods, I love you,' Kamari said affectionately.

''Course you do,' Ellia replied. 'Now keep firing!'

They released their bowstrings as one, the arrows arcing towards their enemy like comets. In desperation, the Kaikru tried to block them with a fresh wall of tendrils, but the flaming arrows forced them to recoil and they found their target anyway. As the Kaikru staggered backwards, tearing at the arrows that scorched his flesh, the wolves saw their opening and took it without hesitation.

'I'll go for the cowl!' Hideo yelled and, before anyone could reply, he had darted around behind the Kaikru.

'Pin his arms!' Jaroe yelled to the others and they rushed to comply, leaping forward as still more flaming arrows rained down upon him. In perfect unison, Jaroe and Kaito pounced at the Kaikru and latched onto his upper arms, bearing him to the ground while Meera and Hina sprang to pin his lower arms.

Behind the Kaikru, Hideo had latched his fangs around the cowl and was tugging at it viciously. Tendrils of dark, oily sickness slid insidiously over his muzzle, but he shut his eyes as he continued to pull with all his might. Achingly slowly, the cowl began to come loose as the Kaikru howled in fury.

'No! No, you cannot...!'

The Kaikru struggled violently but could not break loose – apoplectic with rage and fear. Finally, with one last mighty heave, the cowl came free and Hideo flung it aside. As it hit the ground the cowl began to sizzle, dark clouds springing from its surface as it bubbled and boiled and finally dissolved into the ground. But it was too late for Hideo...

With the Kaikru still breathing, the sickness still lived and in the time it had taken to remove the cowl, the sickness had slipped down Hideo's throat and begun to take hold. Desperate not to succumb, Hideo glanced over at Jaroe, who stared back at him with respect and sorrow. Hideo nodded at him, then turned and flung himself into the fast-flowing river, disappearing beneath the surface without a sound.

With the source of his power gone, the Kaikru grew increasingly more frantic. In his frenzy he bucked like a horse, trying to dislodge them, but they were not letting him get away this time. From between his comrades Takashi leapt onto the Kaikru's chest and stared into his enemy's eyes. For a moment he held his gaze – this twisted creature who had sought to end his world – then, with no words, no preamble, he lowered his head and ripped out his throat with one swift bite.

The Kaikru gurgled, black blood spouting from the wound, his fiery eyes rolling back in his head, but he was not finished yet...

His eyes snapped back into focus, staring directly into Takashi's face, and they narrowed with cold fury. With an almighty effort, he flung the wolves from him and – expending the last of the power that still coursed through his body – placed a hand on the ground where a tendril sprang from his fingertips. With lethal intensity it wove its way past the wolves – past even Kamari and Ellia – towards their house...

As blood poured from his wound and his eyes began to glaze over, the Kaikru's tendril ripped into the foundations of the house, tearing it from the hillside and hefting it aloft like a child's toy. In that moment Takashi saw what was going to happen with perfect clarity. In that moment – for the first time in a long time – he felt he could see and understand the results of each choice before him, free from doubt or uncertainty. One choice led him to the life he had been striving for since his journey began, while the other...

As he stood there frozen, he heard again one of the last things Kamari had said to him before they left Sen'i:

'*I will do what I have to for my loved ones,*' Kamari had said. '*As you always have.*'

As I always have...

It is said that a warrior should come to all decisions in the space of seven breaths... this time, Takashi only needed one...

As the breath died in his throat, the Kaikru hurled the house towards Kamari and Ellia, then collapsed back to the floor and lay still, his tendril dissolving into the ground and vanishing. Kamari and Ellia turned as the shadow fell over them and clutched each other tight, waiting for the inevitable impact.

But it did not come.

Milliseconds before it struck, they felt something bull into them as they clung together, that hurled them out of the path of danger. As Kamari slid to a stop in the mud, he caught a brief glimpse, out of the corner of his eye, of Takashi staring at him from a few paces away. But the strange thing was that it was not Takashi as he was now, but Takashi as he had known him – the boy he had grown up with. There was a sad little smile on his face as he looked at Kamari, but then, in a sudden maelstrom of crashing timber, he was gone.

CHAPTER SEVENTEEN

'Takashi!'

The scream ripped from the throats of both Kamari and Meera, the name spoken in two different tongues but with the self-same shock and fear and grief. Like arrows loosed from bows, they hurtled over to the wreckage through the driving rain and began to dig side by side in the rubble, hurling chunks of wood and stone aside in their frenzy to find him.

As they dug with feverish intensity, they glanced at each other – wishing more than ever before that they could converse to offer words of hope and comfort – but they could not. Once more they were worlds apart, but united in the love of their friend.

They were soon joined by Hina, Kaito, Jaroe and Ellia who leapt to the task of helping shift the mass of twisted timber that had once been a beautiful family home.

As Meera dug, her heart pounded in her ears – each beat a reminder of the precious seconds slipping away. Splinters pierced her, stones cut her, but she did not slow for even a moment.

This cannot be how it ends… she thought. *I cannot lose you like this… Hold on, my love… hold on!*

'Help me with this!' Kamari yelled to Ellia and she sprang to aid him in lifting a huge wooden crossbeam. They strained against it, dust, stones and rainwater pouring all around them – the wolves helping where they could – and finally threw it to one side.

There he was.

Through a narrow aperture in the rubble below he could just about be seen – and he was not moving.

'I'm going in there!' Meera said.

'No! It's unstable!' Hina yelled. 'It could collapse any moment!'

'I don't care!' Meera hurled back as she dived through the opening and wriggled towards her love. Debris creaked and shifted around her as she drew closer and closer and finally made it through to the small, rickety chamber in which Takashi lay in a murky puddle.

'Takashi!' she screamed again as she dived towards him, throwing an ear against his chest to listen for a heartbeat.

Come on, my love… Come on…

She listened, breathing raggedly, hoping against hope to hear the beat of his loyal heart… but as the seconds passed away, no sound reached her ears and she slowly withdrew.

Her world closed in around her, a faint ringing echoing in her head.

No… It cannot be…

But it was.

He was gone… He was gone…

A crash sounded above her and the wreckage shifted.

'Meera!' Jaroe's voice echoed down the aperture. 'You must get out – please!'

Quietly, brokenly, Meera cast one last look at Takashi – her love – then began to squirm her way back out of the tunnel. With only seconds to spare, she tumbled out of the entrance just as the debris fell in on itself with a deafening boom and slowly settled once more.

Kamari looked at Meera – alone and distraught – and fell to his knees.

'No…' he breathed. 'No, no, no…'

Ellia hurried to his side and hugged him tight as the tears began to fall.

'He saved us…' she whispered, as she held onto her husband and joined him in his grief.

Unsteadily, her vision blurred, Meera stumbled away from the wreckage and almost fell with the weight of loss upon her. As the rain continued to pour down, lights began to pop before her eyes, the ringing in her head intensifying. She could not catch her breath, her world shrinking to a pinprick before her, one thought pulsing in her brain: *This is not how it ends… This is not how it ends…*

Vaguely, as though viewing it through a long tunnel, she found herself standing by the body of the Kaikru – the architect of her misery – and loathing welled up inside her. A sound behind made Meera glance around, but she could not tell who it was until she spoke.

'Meera, I… I'm so sorry…' Hina whispered.

'He was the bravest soul I ever knew,' Kaito said, stepping up beside her.

'He will not be forgotten,' Jaroe added. 'He was a warrior through and through.'

'I… I thank you for your words…' Meera said faintly. She swayed on the spot and the others looked on in concern.

'Meera, are you… are you alright…?' Hina asked.

As lights continued to burst before her eyes like fireworks, Meera felt her world begin to spin.

'I don't feel…' Meera began woozily. 'I don't feel so…'

Meera's legs gave way and she began to fall. Time seemed to slow as the rain pelted her and the ground rushed up to meet her.

Without him I cannot go on… the thought eddied and rippled through her unconscious. *Without him, why would I go on…?*

The ringing in her head grew louder; it was deafening now – all-consuming. She squeezed her eyes shut.

I do not want to live in a world without him… I do not want to know that world…

As she finally hit the ground in a spray of mud, she knew at once that something had changed. The rain had stopped, but not only that, it was utterly still and quiet all around her.

Her eyes snapped open and she looked about. It still looked like Kohaku Valley, but different, softer, like a watercolour painting – every object mixing and blending one into another.

She was in Sen'i… But how…?

She got slowly to her feet and turned to see Hina, Kaito and Jaroe standing behind her with the same bewildered expressions as she.

'How…?' Kaito began to ask. 'How did we…?'

A cough to one side made them turn in unison.

'My apologies for doing that without warning,' the voice said. 'But it was me.'

There, kneeling beside the body of the Kaikru, was the Senzo.

'Senzo…' Jaroe murmured, bowing his head respectfully.

'I told you about that before,' the Senzo said with a smile. 'I will not have bowing in my presence – if anything, it is I who should bow to you.'

Jaroe looked up and met eyes with the Senzo.

'I knew you would be the ones to stop this demon,' the Senzo said, turning his attention to the body of the Kaikru. 'You were all meant for this…'

He placed a hand on the Kaikru's chest and looked into the horrific, twisted mask.

'None of us are born bad,' he said softly. 'Sometimes we just make bad choices.'

He closed his eyes and steadied his breathing, and slowly, as the wolves watched in awe, the Kaikru's form changed, the darkness fading away until a young man in the garb of a lord lay before them, his eyes closed peacefully. This was Gen Kichibei as he had once looked before shame and poor choices twisted him.

'You may take him now,' the Senzo said to the empty air. At this, several figures appeared as if from nowhere – the last of Sen'i's Guardians. They lifted Gen's body respectfully and began to bear him away to the north.

'Where will he go...?' Kaito asked quietly. The Senzo did not take his eyes off the body as he replied.

'That is not for you to know yet,' he said. 'But all things find out in time...'

When Gen and the Guardians were lost to view the Senzo turned back to face them.

'You have done this world and your own a great service,' he began, looking at each of them in turn. 'But I know that is not why you originally sought me.'

He turned to face Meera and looked at her piercingly.

'Soul Channel – I know you came to ask something of me,' he said. 'Seeing you now – free from distractions – I believe I know what it is, but I must hear it from you. In return for your great deeds, I will offer you a boon – a single request that I will grant without question. Now... what was it...?'

Meera could barely meet his eyes as the weight of her emotions threatened to crush her. She looked around and saw Jaroe, Hina and Kaito nodding at her encouragingly.

'I... I came here to ask a favour of you...' she began, barely able to speak. 'For... for whatever reason, you saw fit to bestow the gift of the Soul Channel upon me and, while I do not question your judgement, I... I do question myself... I tried to accept this gift, but every part of my being rebelled against it and before I knew what was happening, it... it was killing me... I came here with a request – I was going to ask you to transfer this gift to another, however...' The word hung in the air and Jaroe wrinkled his brow in confusion as she continued. 'I find that I cannot.'

Jaroe stared at her in disbelief at these words.

As Meera stood there, still swaying slightly, she recalled a proverb Takashi had once told her:

A warrior should come to all decisions in the space of seven breaths.

Seven breaths... In that moment Meera found that – for this decision – she only needed one...

'This journey has taken everything from me...' she whispered, her eyes on the floor. 'My Takashi is gone and it... it is not worth living in a world without him...'

She glanced up and met the eyes of the Senzo with resolve and sadness.

'Even if this gift will always keep us separate... even if it means that we can never be, please... if you can... please bring him back... Bring him back and I... I will reject the gift no more. I will accept it wholeheartedly. I will give up the fight – give myself over to it entirely and be your Soul Channel, now and 'til the end of my days...'

The Senzo looked back at her with an expression she could not read.

'If that is what you truly desire...?' he asked slowly.

'It is,' she answered determinedly.

'Then so be it...' the Senzo replied.

The rain had diminished to a fine drizzle as Kamari continued to sift through the rubble with aching arms and bloody knuckles, his kimono sopping wet and sticking to his shaking limbs. Away to the south, the battle between the remaining wolves and spirits still raged as Ellia approached him, her eyes red raw, and put a hand on his arm.

'Dear, it... it is not safe here,' she said gently. 'We... we can continue when the battle is won.'

'No...' Kamari replied brokenly. 'I must find him, I... I cannot leave him under there alone...'

With a mighty effort, he heaved up a huge piece of timber and threw it onto the grass, then stumbled backwards and collapsed to his knees beside Ellia, tears streaking down his face.

'Why...?' he asked, his voice choked. 'Why did he do that...?'

Ellia stroked his hair soothingly.

'He did it for us...' she replied, unable to prevent the break in her voice. 'It was who he was... who he always has been...'

'But he had a chance...' Kamari whispered. 'A chance to finally be with her and he... he chose to give it up...'

'In the end, that's what we are,' Ellia said. 'For better or worse, we are the choices we make… We do not always know what will come of them, all we can do is the best we can…'

Kamari staggered to his feet and looked back at the ruins of his home.

'Then I… I choose to keep digging until I find him,' he said determinedly. 'It is the least I can do…'

Kamari clambered up amongst the wreckage and resumed his search. Ellia watched him sadly for a moment, then headed over to join him. They dug for several minutes in silence, then Kamari stopped.

'I think…' he began. 'I think this is where he was… Help me with this.'

Together, he and Ellia lifted up a chunk of wood and wet paper that had once been the door to their bedroom and heaved it aside to reveal… nothing.

At the base of the hole, where Kamari was sure he had lain, there was no sign of his body, save for a set of wolf prints in the mud.

'Where… where is he…?' Kamari whispered dumbfounded.

'M-Meera…?'

At the sound of that voice she knew and loved so well, Meera turned in elation, and there he was – limping slowly towards her out of the haze from the riverbank.

'Takashi!' she cried, racing towards him and entwining her neck with his before stepping back to look into his eyes – eyes clouded with confusion.

'This is Sen'i…' he began. 'Am I...? Are we…?'

'No…' Meera replied. 'We are alive…'

'But how...?' he whispered. 'How am I…?'

At these words Meera looked away from him. Seeing that she could not meet his eye, Takashi realised what this meant in a trice.

'You didn't...?' he breathed.

'It was the only way to save you,' she said, heartbroken. 'He would grant but one boon, so I… I had to do it – I had to finally give in and accept it…'

'No…' he whispered.

'You get to live…'

'A life without you…'

'And the Council keep their Soul Channel…'

'A life without choice…'

'It was all I could do – please don't be angry.'

'I could never be angry with you – you are everything to me.'

'And you to me.'

'I love you, Meera. I love you more than life itself.'

They became aware in that moment of the Senzo staring at them intently and turned to face him.

'Curious…' he said, to which they looked back at him in bemusement. 'In all my long years, I have rarely seen this before.'

'Seen… what...?' Takashi asked, puzzled.

'There is an old proverb,' the Senzo began. 'It states: "One thing should never become two." I see now that it was written for you... You two are one heart… one soul… one essence… You are meant to be together – were *always* meant to be together – in whatever form that took. Now that I see it, I cannot let this gift come between you any more…'

The Senzo turned to face Hina who looked surprised and anxious at the sudden attention.

'You…' he began, fixing her with an appraising look. 'Hina… I sensed something about you when first we met – a yearning… A desire to help others before ever helping yourself. The gift could pass to none finer than you – though if this experience has taught me anything, it is that this must be *your* decision…'

Takashi, Meera, Kaito and Jaroe all stared at her in awe and amazement as she stood there in a stunned silence. Finally, after what felt like hours, she stepped forward.

'It… it would be the greatest honour of my life,' she said at last, her voice humble.

'Then let us waste no more time…' he replied.

Closing his eyes, the Senzo held his hands up a finger breadth apart and began to rotate them slowly. As they watched, ripples of light seemed to emanate from his palms, growing and spreading, the world appearing to throb and pulse around them like the beating of a heart. The light grew so bright that Takashi, Kaito and Jaroe could no longer bear it and turned away. Then, as suddenly as it had started, it was over, and Meera and Hina lay still on the floor.

'It is done…' the Senzo whispered tiredly.

As though waking from a deep sleep, Meera and Hina got slowly to their feet and looked around them.

'How do you feel...?' Takashi asked Meera nervously, staring into her eyes, but he need not have asked, for he saw the spark of new life dancing deep in their recesses.

'Alive!' she replied breathlessly. 'I feel... truly alive for... for the first time ever!'

Away to their left, Jaroe was staring anxiously at Hina.

'Hina...?' Jaroe began. 'How are you feeling?'

'Ready...' she breathed, brimming with life. 'I feel ready to rebuild our Council.'

Looking around as though seeing everything for the first time, Meera turned to the Senzo, for she had one last question she needed to ask.

'You do not need to answer – but I feel I must ask this anyway...' she began tentatively. 'Why did you choose me as the Soul Channel?'

The Senzo looked at her, a thoughtful smile playing over his lips.

'I think the real question is – if I had not done so, how might all this have played out...?'

Meera glanced away from him and shared a look with Takashi.

'But... how...?' she began to say, but as she turned back, she realised that the Senzo had vanished.

Nearby, Jaroe faced Hina and Kaito and he seemed happier than they had ever seen him.

'I think it is time we return to our Council,' he began, 'for we have a few changes to tell them about. Firstly, of course, of our new Soul Channel, and second...' Here he turned to look at Kaito proudly. 'We must introduce them to the new co-head of our Council.'

Kaito stared back at him agog – hardly able to believe what he had heard.

'Are you…' he whispered falteringly. 'Are you serious…?'

Jaroe nodded firmly.

'I am ashamed to say I thought ill of you for a long time, but you made me realise what I have been missing since Matai's death. I can think of no one else I would rather have by my side at the head of the Council.'

For a moment Kaito struggled to respond.

'I…' he spluttered. 'I am not sure if I am…'

'And that is why it must be you…' Jaroe said. 'A leader without doubt is dangerous. You will make the Council proud – trust me, and trust yourself.'

At these words, Kaito straightened his back and nodded.

'Then I will gladly accept,' he said proudly.

'Good,' Jaroe nodded. 'I have one last thing to do before we go.'

With that, he turned and walked slowly over to Takashi and Meera, taking a seat a few paces from them. They looked at him a little nervously, unsure what to expect.

'I fear this may be a little late, but I… I wanted to apologise,' he began. 'I wanted to apologise for how I have treated you both since you first ran away together. It has taken me a long time to realise this, but… like the Senzo intimated, I believe everything happens for a reason. If you hadn't been chosen and the two of you never fell in love, if you hadn't run away together and the gift hadn't started to wane, then we wouldn't have gone into Sen'i to transfer it, and we may not have found out about the Kaikru's plan until it was too late. However hard it may have been, this was all meant to be, and so I cannot bear a grudge against you and could not see you leave without letting you know that. There will always be a place for you at the Council should you ever wish to visit, though I expect you have other plans...' he finished with a laugh.

Takashi looked back at this wolf he had been through so much with. He had once believed that everything happens for a reason too, but he was not so sure the Senzo's parting words had meant that. To Takashi's mind, what he had truly meant is that – in the end – it all comes down to choice. The Senzo made a choice that led them where they are now – if he had not...

Takashi still fervently believed in a path laid out before all of us – with points along the way we are meant to reach – but he realised then that it is less an exactly planned route and more of a direction. It is your choices – and those of others around you – that define its course, and whether you ever reach those intended destinations. Life is about learning to navigate your path – and those that intersect it – according to your own sense of honour, decency and respect. Some choices you make could lead you from your path, draw you closer to it, or even see you stumble. But as the Senzo had hinted at the waterfall pool, the crucial thing is having the courage to make those choices and learn from the consequences. Whatever the truth of all this, Takashi felt a weight had lifted from him at being reconciled with his friend.

He glanced at Meera and they looked back at Jaroe happily.

'Those words mean more to me than you know,' he said quietly.

'To both of us,' Meera added. 'And we will be sure to visit from time to time.'

'It gladdens my heart to hear this,' Jaroe replied. 'Farewell!'

He nodded at Hina and Kaito and set off south along the riverbank.

'Goodbye,' Kaito called. 'And good luck to you!'

'I will miss you both!' Hina said as she turned away. 'Be safe!'

Together, the three wolves headed south and even from a distance, they could still hear Kaito talking to himself.

'You'll miss them both? Would you miss me if I left? Y'know, I just realised – the Senzo left us in Sen'i... Now we have to go through one of those damn doorways again! I hate those things... He could have dropped us back before he vanished... the nerve of some people!'

Slowly, his voice receded into nothing and Takashi and Meera were finally alone.

'Tell me again,' Takashi said, staring into her eyes. 'How does it feel to be free of it? To finally be free from the will of others?'

Meera looked thoughtful a moment as she pondered this.

'It is like…' she began searchingly. 'It is like I have been beneath a rock my whole life and someone has finally lifted it from me to reveal the sky.'

In that moment it hit Takashi like a wave. It flooded his senses and he revelled in its embrace – he could finally intuit the emotions of another wolf again! He could feel Meera's elation, feel her freedom – unburdened from responsibility or guilt. But in the same moment it hit him, he realised the absence of something. The inevitable feeling – the one that had guided his decisions right up until the Council reclaimed her – had still not returned.

Takashi moved in close and entwined his neck with hers.

'You are all I have ever wanted,' he said. 'All I have ever needed, but I have no idea what happens next. I have no idea what our path is from here…'

'That is the beauty of freedom,' Meera replied happily. 'It is up to us to choose.'

'But… but what if we choose wrong?' he asked uncertainly.

'Then we will be wrong together,' she whispered back.

CHAPTER EIGHTEEN

Excerpt from the journal of Kamari Shiro

It has been much too long since last I wrote in here, but I felt the urge – the *need* – to document everything that occurred after the Kaikru was killed.

So much happened in the moments following his death that my recollection of events is hazy, but I will relate what I remember as best I can.

It was a strange and sudden parting from my comrades after Takashi fell. Meera, Jaroe, Kaito and Hina – as well as the corpse of the Kaikru – vanished without a trace while I searched for my friend's body and the battle with the spirits continued to rage, but it did not go on for long…

Shortly after the Kaikru died his dark clouds parted and dissipated, leaving in their wake a clear sky that spoke of hope for the future. Without his influence, the sick spirits still locked in combat with the remaining wolves were set free and it was a sight to behold. Like watching a sunrise cresting the horizon, they each returned to their original forms in a dazzling gleam of light and drifted back to the doorways to Sen'i, where they could finally complete the Pilgrimage.

With the battle over, the remainder of the Council stayed long enough to check that we were alright, but without a common tongue to converse in, there was little to be done. With a nod and a wave, we bade our farewells and they disappeared south along the western riverbank to return to their quarry. It saddened me to see how few remained of that brave and noble race, and I hoped against hope that Meera had been able to transfer the gift, so she could save both herself and the remnants of the Council.

However, I did not have long to dwell on these thoughts. I needed to ensure that the Senzo's assertion – that killing the Kaikru would cure the infected and stop the spread – was indeed true. In the chaos of the past few hours, I had forgotten that *I* was one of those infected. I rolled up my sleeve and was disconcerted to discover that the black nodules had not disappeared – was I still infected, or would it clear in time...?

Wearily, with Ellia by my side, we hurried south down the eastern riverbank and soon found the villagers – cold, wet and scared – amassed at the Valley Spirit shrine, praying for deliverance. Ellia and I went round each of the infected but, as with myself, it was not immediately clear whether the loss of the Kaikru's influence had had any impact on their health at all.

I explained the situation – told them what I knew, what I believed – and it was enough to kindle the spark of hope in them once more that things could get better. Slowly, due to numbers and ill health, we made our way back up the valley to the village and there were cries of consternation at the destruction wrought by the Kaikru and his army. Tears were shed at the loss of the bridge – for it had been a fixture of the village for generations – but far more precious things than wood and stone had been lost that night and there would be much grieving to come.

The following few days were some of the most tense and nerve-wracking of my life as we waited to see whether the infected – including myself – would get better, as I had promised they would. The first hopeful sign was that there were no new cases over the second and third day and then, finally, by the fourth day, I both saw and felt the improvements in our health, and at last I knew for certain that we would make it.

In the space of two weeks, all the infected had returned to full health, but the timing of the Kaikru's death had been too late for some. When I left Aigano to find the source of the sickness, only Tayo had died, but between then and the battle we lost a dozen more good, honest souls to the Kaikru's cruelty. Those who perished were mainly very young or very old, but one miracle in all this was that Mara – the young girl who was infected around the same time as Tayo – miraculously survived, fighting off the infection with a will of iron. It is clear to me that she will go far in this world.

Once myself and the rest had adequately recuperated from our ordeal, we held a ceremony to honour the dead. As was customary, their bodies were burnt to ash before being buried in the small cemetery at the northern end of the village. Following this sombre affair, we concluded with a celebration – not only to commemorate those we lost – but to revel in the knowledge that the sickness had passed and to thank the wolves for their great sacrifice on behalf of the entire Hirono Domain.

The celebration lasted two days and nights and was an absolute joy to behold. After witnessing the fear, suspicion, isolation and separation the sickness had instilled in the villagers, it was wonderful to see them mingling together again, shaking hands and laughing like they had not a care in the world.

But, being the village leader, it was my job to remind them that life is not all fun and games! While the battle had largely taken place on the western bank, there was still some damage done to buildings on the eastern side. Boulders hurled by the Kaikru had destroyed a grain store, a well and a woodshed – but the largest amount of work required was on the bridge, and my house…

Sifting through the wreckage of my home as we began to rebuild was a strange and disconnected experience. Ellia and I had lived there ever since we moved back after the battle with Zian, and as we sorted through the debris, it reminded me just how much of my parents' belongings still remained in our family home. After much discussion, we decided not to rebuild it exactly as it was, but to build something more suited to our needs and our tastes. It is important to honour the past, but not to be bound by it.

But the part of our plan that really shocked the villagers was our decision to rebuild on the eastern bank, alongside the rest of the housing. The ancestral homes of the Asano and Shiro families had been deliberately built on the western bank to mark them out as different from the common villagers, but that was no longer the way I wanted to live – the way I wanted to be viewed by my people. And so, we rebuilt alongside them and shifted the home of Mia and Takashi's mother – with their blessing of course – over to the eastern bank as well.

Before all this, however, we needed to rebuild the bridge to allow passage from one bank to the other. As with my home, we decided not to rebuild it exactly as it was. What we created instead was something bigger and more functional, but to honour the saviours of our village, our best carpenters went all-out on carving beautiful wolf-inspired designs for the railings that told the tale of their triumph over the Kaikru.

Throughout all of this, Takashi's young sister Mia was an instrumental force. Everybody in the village wanted to pitch in with the rebuilds, including the children, and Mia organised them into an efficient unit that put the adults to shame. My two children are only young, but they already look up to her like an idol. As with Mara, I see great things in her future and strongly believe she would be an excellent village leader one day.

In the wake of our battle with the Kaikru, Ellia has made great plans for Aigano to truly become the outpost of Harakima it was meant to be, since she moved here after being made a Kurai. It was something I had always planned to do, but she has gripped the bull by the horns and taken on the challenge of training up our own fighting force so that in future, we will be able to defend ourselves, and not have to rely on others. I did not think it was possible to love her more than I already do, but somehow my love for her grows daily.

The hour is getting late and I have my duties to attend to, but there is of course one last topic I have barely touched on that I must address – the loss of my friend, my brother, Takashi Asano. The moment I had to tell his mother – a moment I had already been through once before – was one of the worst of my entire life, and the fact that we could not even provide a body made it so much harder. But I will never forget what she said when I told her he had passed:

'Has he now...' she had said. This was then followed by a cryptic: 'We shall see...'

I should have known to trust her instincts – to trust him – for she was right to be sceptical. One day, several months later, I was awoken by a howl outside my bedroom window and, with Ellia by my side, we stepped out on to the veranda to investigate… and there they were. Takashi and Meera stood side-by-side on the grass outside our home and I had never seen them looking happier or healthier. Although we could not converse, they had clearly come to check up on us and show us they were alive and well. But, more than this – and to my great joy – they had come to proudly show us their new arrivals…

EPILOGUE

The moon gazed down out of a starless sky, illuminating their way as they ran side-by-side – Meera, Takashi and their three new cubs. The cubs were still only young, but already they could run as though full grown and Takashi's heart swelled with pride to see it. In that moment the air had never smelled sweeter, the grass had never felt softer, the night sky had never looked more beautiful, and Takashi and Meera had never been happier.

For the first time in their lives they were truly free. Takashi found himself free from the inevitable feeling – both its presence and then its loss. He would never know where it had come from, but he recognised it now as intention, not inevitability – a guiding hand that had helped him along his path right up until the Council reclaimed Meera. Throughout his whole adventure since, he had made his way without it, and he realised in that moment that that is precisely what it had prepared him to do. For Meera, there was no longer anyone above her to control her actions or dictate her life – no one to make her choices for her.

Whatever may have been intended for them along the way, they both knew that – at last – they were finally where they were meant to be. For better or worse, their lives were now their own and ahead of them lay a whole world of choices – both good and bad, successes and mistakes – for them to make. They would stumble along the way, they wouldn't always get things right, but as long as they were together and as long as those choices were theirs and theirs alone, then they would be happy. But for now, they were content to simply run, as they had always wanted to do, and see where their legs would take them and what fresh choices they would find along the way...